Only the Cat Knows

Only the Cat Knows

. . .

MARIAN BABSON

Thomas Dunne Books

ST. MARTIN'S MINOTAUR

NEW YORK

THOMAS DUNNE BOOKS.
An imprint of St. Martin's Press.

www.thomasdunnebooks.com
www.minotaurbooks.com

Library of Congress Cataloging-in-Publication Data

Babson, Marian.
    Only the cat knows / Marian Babson.—1st U.S. ed.
        p. cm.
    ISBN-13: 978-0-312-33238-9
    ISBN-10: 0-312-33238-6
    1. Women cat owners—Fiction. 2. Attempted murder—Fiction.
3. Amnesia—Fiction. I. Title.

PS3552.A25 O55 2007
813'.54—dc22

JUN 1 8 2007   2007009537

First published as *Only the Cat* in the UK by Constable,
an imprint of Constable & Robinson Ltd 2007

First U.S. Edition: June 2007

10 9 8 7 6 5 4 3 2 1

Prologue

I awoke in excruciating pain, unable to tell where it began or ended. Every bone was broken, every ligament torn, every internal organ wrenched out of place. Everything – everything – smashed beyond repair. The thin envelope of skin was pierced in a hundred places, the blood pulsing out to seep into the cold damp ground.

Bitch! The venomous hatred in the explosive whisper seared my eardrums, bringing more pain. Who hated me that much?

I forced my eyes open and for a brief hallucinatory moment I saw a wall of earth, felt a trickle of icy water beneath me, was aware of the ivy-clad tower of an ancient building looming into the dark sky above me . . .

No . . . not me.

The vision began to fade. I closed my eyes and opened them again. I was lying in bed in a Melbourne hotel at the end of a hugely successful Australian tour. I was safe, warm, comfortable.

The pain was retreating into just a memory of pain, the last residue of an exceptionally vivid nightmare.

Or was it?

Panic was surging in to replace the earlier sensations. Panic – and a dark foreboding.

It was a strange thing being a twin, sometimes we each seemed one-half of a whole. Blood of my blood, bone of my bone, the tie was stronger in a way than mere direct lineage, than even the parent–child relationship.

It meant that there was always someone there, a mind

5

that meshed with your own. Someone to laugh with, share secrets with, always there, with reactions identical to your own. It meant you were never alone, in the way other people were.

It was a privileged life that carried with it a secret dread: by the very nature of life, of mortality, it could not go on for ever. Some day one or the other of us would have to pay.

No! It had just been a nightmare. It was something I ate. It wasn't true.

I tried to keep fighting as the swirling vortex carried me down into sleep – or unconsciousness – but, deep down, I knew.

Something terrible had just happened to Nessa.

Chapter One

At least she was still alive. If only just.

I stared down at the supine motionless form, cocooned in bandages, sustained by tubes and wires. I couldn't see her breathing, but the flickering line on the display panel of one of the battery of machines at her bedside appeared to be monitoring her respiration.

She was getting the best medical attention that money could buy. Her employer could do no less. He'd better not.

I took a step closer, but did not need the warning gesture from the young doctor to restrain me. I wasn't going to touch her. I was afraid to. She looked so fragile – a shattered doll that had been jigsawed back into a semblance of its former shape, but which might disintegrate beyond restoration if breathed on too heavily.

'Hi there, Nessa.' I settled for vocal contact instead, in the voice we so nearly shared. 'Your other half is here. It's going to be all right now.'

The doctor glanced at me quickly and then glanced away again. He didn't contradict me, but his expression was not optimistic.

'You're going to be all right now.' I spoke with more firmness than I felt. My knees were turning to jelly, something twisted in the pit of my stomach. She was so pale . . . so still.

'What happened?' I asked. The garbled message that had reached me had told me little. Only that she needed me. I had abandoned my plans for a leisurely sea voyage back to England and caught the first jet instead.

'She fell from a considerable height, I understand. I'm told she was in the habit of wandering along the battlements when she couldn't sleep at night. She must have missed her footing.'

'Whoever told you that was . . . mistaken. She was afraid of heights. She'd never have done that.' It was one of the few points where we diverged. Heights didn't bother me. But she had been afraid with good reason, it seemed now. Had that fear been a presentiment of what lay in her future?

'Well . . .' His face shadowed, he pointed out the irrefutable. 'It happened. She's lucky the patrol dogs found her in the dry moat beneath the battlements. Otherwise, she might have lain there all night. That would have . . .' He let the thought trail off. I could finish the sentence for myself.

'At least she has a fighting chance now.' I wasn't going to give up and I knew that she wouldn't.

'We'll do our best.' Against my will, I identified the expression that flitted across his face: it was pity.

'She'll be all right,' I said. 'She's a fighter.' And so am I. I wanted to know how this could have happened to her.

'Er . . .' He cast a worried glance at the information registering on the various screens. 'It might be better if we left her to rest now.' He led the way outside.

'She's going to be all right,' I insisted. 'There are two of us fighting now.'

'You know . . .' He assessed me carefully. 'You're not what I expected.'

'I know,' I said. 'I'm never what anyone expected. But enough of me. Nessa is the important one here. What else is being done for her? Are there any specialists we can call in? Does she need a blood transfusion? We match, of course.'

'Everything possible is being done. Mr Oversall has seen to that. It's a question of time now.'

'And does Mr Oversall know that? I rang his office for information as soon as I got to London. They didn't give me the impression that Nessa's condition was serious at all. They made it sound as though they expected her back at work in a couple of days.'

'Ah, yes.' He looked embarrassed. 'Our Mr Oversall is notoriously optimistic. He's had to be – or he wouldn't be where he is today.'

One of the richest men in the world. Notorious, indeed, for investing in schemes wiser men shunned, like backing dubious freedom fighters in areas of upheaval, or buying up mineworkings popularly supposed to be exhausted which subsequently turned out to have hidden resources unsuspected by the owners who had sold them to him. A lucky man – or one with impeccable sources of information.

'People tend to tell Mr Oversall what he wants to hear.' He was apologetic. 'I'm the junior doctor in this practice. I couldn't contradict what the senior partner said.'

The man who pays the piper is the man who calls the tune. And Mr Oversall paid well. But what would he say if the tune became discordant, the music jangled . . . the patient died?

I wasn't going to let myself think that but, just for a moment, I faltered.

'I won't deny I'm not entirely happy,' he went on. 'I . . . I've met Nessa . . . several times. I . . . I liked her. I'd formed the opinion that she was a calm and sensible person – unlike most of Mr Oversall's . . .'

'Harem.' I supplied the word he had baulked at. It had been used often enough in the tabloids. The more discreet broadsheets usually opted for 'Amazon Army' to describe the plethora of nubile females surrounding the billionaire.

'I wasn't suggesting your sister –'

'I should hope not! Nessa was – is – a proper employee. Mr Oversall's Personal Assistant. She has no connection with the . . . the ladies . . . who make up his entourage.'

'Exactly!' He nodded vehemently. 'Nessa is different . . . special . . .'

'Exactly!' I nodded in turn, beginning to wonder about his relationship with my twin. Interested? Smitten? Or . . .? 'I think I'd like to have a few words with your senior partner,' I said.

'Unfortunately, that's not possible.' He was on the defensive again. 'I mean, Dr Ranjit is out on a call. I don't know when he'll be back.'

'I can wait.'

'I doubt it. He's on his way to Saudi Arabia. There's been some sort of outbreak at one of the installations. They're hoping to avoid an epidemic.'

'I take it the installation belongs to Mr Oversall.' It wasn't a question.

'Right. Our . . . our practice . . . is largely . . . er . . . involved . . . with Oversall Enterprises. We have very few National Health or private patients.'

Why was I not surprised? It all made perfect sense. Of course, Mr Oversall would maintain his own medical unit for his far-flung empire. So much easier than having to deal with all the local regulations, restrictions and native doctors.

'And I suppose the police have not been informed about Nessa's . . . accident?' It was another question to which I already knew the answer.

'Police?' He recoiled. 'What have they to do with it? They aren't automatically called to the scene of every accident. Our own paramedics got there faster than any other ambulance could have. I assure you, she's having the best of care.'

'Of course.' Just as I had suspected. No names, no pack drill . . . no record. Whatever had happened was going to be swept under the carpet – a very expensive, highest-quality Oriental carpet, but a carpet nonetheless. Whatever had happened to her, for whatever reason, was going to be swept away. Lost, as she might be . . .

'I want to know what happened,' I said. 'From the very beginning.'

'I wouldn't mind knowing myself,' he admitted. 'If she recovers enough to tell us . . .'

'No.' I stood there, all my energy concentrated on sending out a mental call to Nessa to respond. It had often worked in the past, no matter how far apart we had been. Not this time. She was too far away, whatever spark she had was curled up in the centre of her being, fighting to survive, to return to life. She needed all her own energy for that. I cut off the signal, it wasn't fair to ask her to dissipate any energy that was left to her.

'No.' I stood there, limp and empty but for a growing rage. 'I can't wait that long.'

'And even if . . . when . . . she recovers consciousness –' he was having trouble treading the line between honesty and optimism; just as well Mr Oversall wasn't here – 'we don't know how much brain damage there might be. There's usually short-term memory loss in cases like this, especially about events just before the accident. She may never be able to tell you anything about it.'

'Amnesia . . .' I said. 'Temporary amnesia.'

'It might be permanent,' he warned.

Somewhere in the back of my mind, I had known that: read it, heard it, learned it in some long-ago psychology course. A plan began to form in my mind. Or had it been there all along?

'Have you mentioned this to anyone at Friary Keep?'

'Not really.' He looked uncomfortable. 'No one's asked. Apart from Mr Oversall, of course, and my senior partner handled that . . . before he went away.'

'Poor Nessa . . .' There had been vague intimations in some of her letters. *Bitch!* The echo of that hateful whisper surfaced faintly in my mind. 'Not very popular, was she?'

'No one was.' His mouth twisted wryly. 'It's everyone for themselves in that set-up. Nothing to take personally.'

'A strange ménage.' He couldn't deny it. 'So no one

11

knows, or particularly cares about, the actual position. Except for the optimistic Mr Oversall, who is expecting Nessa back on duty in very short order.'

'I'm afraid that sums it up.'

'And now your senior has gone away and you're the one left to tell Mr Oversall the unpalatable truth.'

'Yes.' He knew it. He'd known it all along, but he didn't like having it pointed out to him.

'Mr Oversall isn't going to like it.'

'No, but they don't kill the messenger any more.' His uncertain smile said he wished he could be sure of that.

'I wouldn't bet on it.' Shamelessly, I preyed on his fears. 'I understand Mr Oversall can be quite nasty when thwarted.'

'One hears rumours.' He lost a little more colour. 'But even a billionaire has to face reality occasionally.' Mortality, he meant.

'Not necessarily. I think we should send Nessa back to him. A little the worse for wear, perhaps, and not quite up to the job for a while longer. In need of rest – but able to learn quite a lot while she takes her time recovering.'

'What do you mean? She can't possibly be moved. You've seen –' He broke off, looking at me with growing – and justified – suspicion.

'I'll take her place. We're twins, remember.'

'But – but – you can't!'

'With your help, I can. Just make sure everyone knows that I'm suffering from amnesia. I think we'll make that total amnesia, not just the short-term kind.'

'But –'

I smiled. The gowns, the wigs, the glitter, the glamour that comprised my stage persona, Gloriana, were all packed away in the theatrical trunks following me in the hold of the liner I had intended to sail in, but who needed them? I half-turned, moistened my lips and gave him a smouldering look.

'You – you're –' He choked.

'Go ahead, say it.' I shrugged languorously. 'I've been

called obscene before.' It was his own reaction that had shocked him, I knew. That split second in which he had felt the pull, glimpsed the dark side of the moon.

'I didn't mean that,' he said. 'I mean, you'll never get away with it!'

'Oh, yes, I will!' I dropped the coquetry and let my face reveal the depth of my fury – and my determination. Someone had tried to kill Nessa and I intended to find out who. 'All you have to do is sell them the amnesia story. You can do that, can't you?'

'Yes, but – you –' He shook his head. 'You're –'

'I'll tell you what I am,' I snapped. 'Twindom apart, I'm the best damned female impersonator in the business!'

Chapter Two

The guard dogs began baying as the car swung through the wrought-iron gates and up the long curving tree-lined drive. I knew, from Nessa's letters, that the kennels were sited along the outer wall, the better to discourage prospective trespassers. At night, the dogs were freed to roam the grounds – except for the more dangerous ones, who patrolled with the armed guards.

Friary Keep lurched, rather than sprawled, across the top of the low hill like a mad Disneyland extravaganza. At one end, a tower masquerading as a Norman keep rising out of a moat stood guard over a terraced conglomeration of buildings, starting with a medieval manor, which blended into a half-timbered Tudor town house, which melded in turn into a red-brick mullion-windowed Elizabethan manor. At the very end, standing on its own in another moat, a Gothic tower balanced the arrangement. I wondered which tower Nessa had fallen – or been pushed – from.

'The cloisters are around at the back,' Dr Anderson said, as he drove around the end of the tower. 'That's where they have the guest rooms and the superior staff quarters. You have a small suite of your own.' He had refused the offer of a chauffeur to collect me and elected to drive me himself, so that I could have a last-minute briefing. The amnesia could account for anything he had missed.

'Where are the inferior staff quarters?'

'In the Norman tower,' he answered seriously. 'The Gothic tower is just for show. A folly, really.'

'It all looks like a folly to me. It must be like living in an architectural historian's nightmare.'

'It's all a Victorian fake,' he assured me. 'But it's been brought right up to date. Behind the pseudo-period features, it's all mod cons and the latest technology. You can sit in the anchorite's cell one minute and surf the Internet the next.'

'There's a cell, too?'

'What cloister would be without something so atmospheric? I understand the original Victorian owner even had a wax dummy installed – which looked so real it frightened the servants. Except for the butler, who decided the cell was an ideal place to commit suicide and was discovered hanging there in the robes he'd stripped from the dummy. After that, rumours began that the place was haunted.'

'It was a superstitious age,' I said absently. Heat-sensitive lights had blazed into life as we drew up in front of an iron-studded heavy oak door. Something moved behind the small glass panel at one side and the door swung open as we got out of the car.

'Vanessa?' The figure was shadowy with the light behind her, but her voice seemed warm and concerned. I braced myself for my first hurdle.

'Mrs Chandler, the housekeeper,' Dr Anderson cued me softly.

He meant well, but I ignored the information. If I greeted her by name, the idea might get around that my amnesia was not so complete as someone might have hoped. Memory had to return gradually – if at all.

'Vanessa!' She stopped short of embracing me, noting my obvious fragility. 'I'm so glad you're back. How are you?'

'I'm not sure . . .' I smiled vaguely at the maternal figure.

'I'm afraid . . . she's a long way from being . . . her old self,' Dr Anderson said carefully, making sure he was using the correct pronoun.

15

'I understand.' She nodded, accepting the hesitancy as his delicacy in offering any sort of diagnosis in front of the patient. 'You'll do better, now that we have you back home, my dear. We'll have you on your feet in no time.'

'Thank you, Ms . . .?' I might as well hammer it home right from the beginning.

'Oh!' Her hand fluttered up to her heart, she looked across me to the doctor. 'I – I knew, of course. I – I supposed I hadn't really understood –'

'Vanessa, this is Monica Chandler, the housekeeper.' He introduced me formally. 'She'll take good care of you.' He met the woman's anxious eyes. '*And* she'll introduce you to the others,' he underlined.

'Oh . . . yes. Yes, of course.' She was out of her depth. She'd obviously had to deal with a great many problems during her long domestic career, but never anything like this before. 'I'm sorry.'

'So am I.' Smiling weakly, I swayed against Dr Anderson, who tensed slightly before ostentatiously offering his arm.

'Perhaps we should get her to her quarters,' he said. 'She ought to lie down now.'

'Of course.' She led the way along a corridor lit by electric candles which flickered realistically and didn't give off enough light to illuminate the dark corners. Atmospheric was the obvious intention. 'Spooky,' Nessa had called it in one of her letters to me.

Her letters – why had I thrown so many of them away so blithely? Three moves are as good as a fire, they say, and I was always on the move. True, most of our correspondence had been frittered into cyberspace but, when she was really disturbed, Nessa found the old-fashioned pen-to-paper routine the best therapy for her anxiety. I should have paid more attention to her fears.

Somewhere behind us, I caught the sound of a door opening and closing quietly. Someone taking a furtive peek at the returning outpatient?

'Here we are!' We had reached the end of the cloister

and another iron-bound oak door blocked our way. Monica Chandler pulled a key from her pocket and turned it in the lock. 'Here are your quarters!' She swung the door wide, giving me a hopeful look, as though the sight of my private domain might instantly restore my memory and we could all have a good laugh.

Although she stepped aside to allow me to enter, I remained where I was, taking stock of my surroundings. The door opened directly into a pleasant L-shaped sitting room. The short end of the L cut across the end of the cloister and seemed to be a sort of office, while the long main room stretched along the cloister with doors on the opposite wall flanking a fireplace. There were deep over-stuffed armchairs and sofa, with floor lamps positioned behind them for comfortable reading, a small but well-filled bookcase in a corner and fresh flowers in a crystal vase on a polished end table.

I was aware that Monica Chandler was watching my face closely – and that it gave nothing away. After a moment, she gave a tiny shrug and stepped across the threshold herself, leading the way. I followed.

'And here's Gloriana!' she cried, flinging out one hand dramatically.

I froze. The intonation and gesture were a parody of the usual introduction to my act. Had I been unmasked already?

'Come to welcome you home!' she concluded and I followed the line of her gesture to find myself looking down at a dainty white Angora cat with sapphire eyes. I stared at it, still frozen, unable to move despite a nudge from Dr Anderson urging me forward.

'No!' Monica Chandler said with disbelief. 'You mean she doesn't even remember her beautiful little cat? I can't believe it!'

Neither could I. The cat and I stared at each other blankly. It lifted its head and sniffed in my direction, the tip of its tail twitched ominously, the sapphires turned to chips of blue ice.

No rapturous reunion here. Monica was visibly disappointed.

'Look, Gloriana,' she urged. 'Mummy's home!'

The cat gave me a frigid *Have we been introduced?* stare, as affronted as a Dowager Duchess who had just had her bottom pinched by a passing street person. Then she turned her back on us, sat down and began to wash her face. At least she hadn't run away.

'That's cats for you.' Dr Anderson tried to retrieve the situation. 'When they think you've been neglecting them, they'll make you pay for it.'

'It must be the hospital smell.' I touched the bandage discreetly peeping from beneath my turban and spoke very softly, as befitted my bruised throat. 'It reminds her of the vet.'

'That must be it,' Monica agreed.

'I shan't try to make it up with her right now.' I gave a weary sigh. 'I'm too tired . . .'

'You must be exhausted!' Monica was good at picking up a cue. 'I've turned your bed down and it's all ready for you. Go straight to bed and get some sleep. I'll bring you breakfast in the morning. Just give me a ring on the intercom when you're ready for it.'

'How kind of you,' I murmured.

'Not at all.' She gave me a worried look. 'It's my job.' She was at the door now, but hesitated. 'You're sure you're all right?'

'Pretty much so.' I smiled faintly at her. 'Just terribly tired.'

'Keep taking the tablets.' Anderson winked at me as Monica turned away. He was getting braver now that escape was in sight.

'Don't worry, I will.' I followed them to the door and opened it like a good hostess.

'Be careful.' He was serious again. 'Any problems, phone me immediately. You have my number.'

'We'll take good care of her,' Monica said. 'We'll call you instantly if – But there shouldn't be –'

18

'I'm sure I'll sleep through until morning.' I began closing the door on them. 'Perhaps even until noon.'

'Sleep as long as you like –' Monica began.

'Thank you both. So much.' I closed the door firmly and listened to their retreating footsteps. After a tactful interval, I turned the key in the lock and noticed that there was also a large brass bolt attached to the door.

It looked new. Too bright and shiny to match the original dark lock and doorknob. Furthermore, the wood surrounding it looked scratched and raw, as though the bolt had been affixed recently.

Wishing I had paid more attention to Nessa's most recent letters – or had had the ability to read between the uneasy lines – I slid the bolt home. It couldn't do any harm and I didn't want anyone popping in on me unexpectedly. I'd open it in the morning before breakfast arrived so that there wouldn't be any wounded feelings.

That decided, I took a deep breath and decided to make myself more comfortable. But first . . . I crossed to the window looking out on to the cloister walkway and checked to make sure it was locked. It was and I was pleased to discover that, lurking behind the curtains, heavy wooden shutters were there to be secured across the window. Interesting, because they were out-of-period, but suggested that security took precedence over authenticity.

Authenticity? Anderson had said the whole pseudo-kingdom was just a big Victorian fake. And the shutters had obviously been part of the original fittings, they were a lot older than the brass bolt on the door – but would be just as effective in keeping out marauders.

I locked them in place, then drew the curtains across, concealing them, and repeated the process for the office window which also faced on to the walkway.

A quick look into the other rooms revealed narrow windows so high up that no one outside could possibly see in. Why, then, did I have the feeling I was being watched?

Because I was. I turned back into the sitting room to find the cat perched on an arm of the sofa, watching me intently as I prowled around. I nodded to her and she looked away quickly.

'All right, be like that.' I removed my turban and eased off the bandages that had been stitched together into a sort of helmet so that I needn't try to wrap and unwrap the long length of bandage by myself.

I tossed the headgear on to the nearest chair, followed it with my kaftan and padded bra, then treated myself to a long luxurious scratch of the stubble on my head. The doctor and I had agreed that a close crop rather than a shaven head would offer more camouflage in case the bandage-helmet slipped. In the few seconds before I could adjust it, the stubble would help conceal the fact that there were no wounds visible.

The cat was staring openly at me now. It was obvious that she had never seen a jockstrap before. I hadn't known that cats could look askance.

I turned off the lights in the sitting room and headed back to the bedroom to find out where Nessa kept her nightgowns. The bed had been turned down and the crisp white sheets yawned invitingly. I yawned, too, suddenly aware that I was as exhausted as though I'd genuinely been released from hospital that evening. Walking on egg-shells, trying not to put a foot wrong, takes a lot out of you.

Someone else was walking delicately, too. She hesitated in the doorway, her eyes wide and wary.

'Gloriana –' I said to my namesake. 'Come in and let's get acquainted. If we can't make friends fast, you're going to get me in trouble.'

She advanced into the room a few steps, then something behind her caught her attention. She turned back, her fur bristling, her gaze fixed on something out of my range of vision.

'What's the matter?' Her anxiety was contagious. 'Not seeing ghosts, are you?'

Ignoring me, she lowered her body to an inch above the floor and half-slunk, half-stalked into the sitting room.

Uneasily, I followed her, looking around to see what had spooked her.

Everything was as I had left it. No wisps of ectoplasm were visible in the dim light filtering into the room from the bedroom. I collected the helmet, turban, bra and kaftan from the chair to take back into the bedroom with me. I'd need them when Monica brought my breakfast tray.

I wondered whether I should pick up the cat, too, or whether I'd have a battle on my hands if I tried. Some cats don't take kindly to being handled by strangers. Better not.

While I was still watching her thoughtfully, she turned and looked over her shoulder at me. Her mouth opened in a vehement hiss.

Decidedly better not. Then I followed her gaze as she turned her head away and realized that the hiss had not been directed at me, but was a comment on our situation.

The doorknob of the outer door was silently turning.

There was also a faint scrabbling sound. A key twisting in the lock? But the bolt held.

The door began shaking as a certain amount of force was applied to it, still very quietly. Someone was determined to get in – and didn't want anyone to know it.

Gloriana and I moved closer together. I felt my top lip curl back as I instinctively mimicked her silent hiss. It seemed the only fitting response at the moment.

'Darling – it's me!' The shaking changed to a light tapping. 'I know you're in there. Are you all right? I must see for myself.' It was a deep male voice, plummy with faintly theatrical overtones.

'Beloved –' The voice lowered seductively. 'Beloved, let me in.'

Chapter Three

Not by the hair on your chinny-chin-chin!

I backed away from the door. Gloriana backed with me, still glaring at the door. Whoever was on the other side of it was not on her list of favourite people. We were as one on that.

'Darling?' The insistent voice began to falter. 'Are you awake?'

Who was this man? And how much else was there that Nessa hadn't told me?

Quite a lot, obviously. Perhaps she had planned to tell me all about it when I arrived. And yet . . . and yet . . . I had had no flash of intuition to tell me that she was emotionally involved. Was that because the essential closeness of twinship was breached when True Love entered the equation?

I wouldn't know. Whatever brief encounters had come my way had been amusing and, in their way, fulfilling, but nothing that could be categorized as True Love. Not yet.

'Darling . . .' He was giving up. Perhaps he felt too exposed, standing at the near end of the cloister, tapping on an unyielding door. 'Sleep well, then. Until the morrow. I'll be busy all day, but the night . . . the night will be our own!'

That's what you think!

Morrow? The night will be our own? Who was this ham? What was Nessa doing tied up with him? Had she lost her sense of humour – or her mind?

Whoever he was, Romeo was not going to be the one to

make any dent in my amnesia. He was going straight back to being a stranger – and staying there. So far as I was concerned, we had not been introduced.

On the other hand, Gloriana and I appeared to be bonding after our experience with the voice on the other side of the door. Clearly, she approved of my not letting him in. I felt soft fur brush my ankle lightly as we returned to the bedroom. She was the only one I was going to share it with tonight.

Sleep . . .? I lay there staring into darkness. How could I have imagined, even for one insane moment, that sleep would be possible? In a strange bed . . . in a strange house . . . surrounded by strangers?

And isn't that a definition of any hotel you've ever stayed in? The reasonable side of my brain tried to calm me.

Not quite. I would not be soothed. In this place, one of the strangers was an enemy. Perhaps more than one. And who knew what else one or more of them might be?

How many of them were there? What were they to Nessa? Or she to them? This was the first time she had ever taken on a residential job. Had she been enjoying it – or had she begun to regret it?

I turned over restlessly and punched a dent in the pillow. It was too dark here, too quiet. At least, in a hotel, there were sounds of life around you. Normal life. Loud voices, laughter, the boom of a television set, an occasional snatch of drunken song . . . and unashamed footsteps noisily heading towards their rightful room.

I found myself listening again for the furtive steps shuffling outside my door. Stupid, of course. Beloved had long since drifted away to his own lair. Secrecy seemed to be paramount; he would not want anyone to catch him loitering outside Nessa's quarters.

Outside, there were the sounds of the night. The wind rising, a splatter of rain – good, that would discourage any other incipient prowlers. In the distance, guard dogs barked . . . except for the one that howled. Another splatter of rain told me there was no moon for it to howl at.

Night has a thousand sounds . . . and a thousand eyes. I could feel them watching me now. For an uneasy moment, I wondered whether there was a spyhole in one of the walls . . . or a hidden camera.

A faint whisper of sound, close by, and I turned to find that the cat was crouching in the bedside armchair and was watching me intently . . . suspiciously.

'Oh, come along,' I said, patting the bed. 'Come over and let's get acquainted.'

Oooops! I had offended the Dowager Duchess again. Her head reared back, her eyes went icy. The temporary truce that had ensued when I ignored Beloved was over. We were back on barely nodding terms again.

'All right, be like that.' I turned over. 'See if I care.'

But I did. If we couldn't reach a semblance of amity, if not intimacy, she might blow my cover. In her current amnesiac condition, 'Nessa' might not remember her cat, but the cat would be expected to recognize and welcome Nessa. A loving cat can only maintain a snit at her mistress for a limited time. If the Duchess didn't come round soon, I could be in trouble.

They say you never have a really sleepless night, it's just an illusion; that, actually, you have a series of catnaps in between the periods of wakefulness. It's because the wakefulness is so clear and worrying that it seems never to have ended.

Perhaps I did sleep, after all. At some point, I must have drifted off. Suddenly, the room was noticeably brighter, the cat was gone from the armchair, and there were faint sounds of the world moving back into action in the distance. A car motor roared, a dog barked – a different kind of dog – not the deep menacing snarling bark of the guard dogs, this sounded like a more normal dog, one you might be able to reason with. Some sort of bird cried out plaintively . . . a seagull? How near the sea were we?

No point in lying here any longer. Time to get up and

face what the day might bring. Face . . . yes, a quick close shave first thing, before anyone came calling, and a light application of foundation cream, dappled with a judicious overlay of darker shades to simulate fading bruises.

That accomplished, I did a quick survey of what was available in Nessa's wardrobe. Luckily, we were both tall and had the same build, typical twins. The fit would be no problem.

Especially with the full-length kaftans we both loved. I knew she had a full wardrobe of them – I had provided it myself. My early years as an entertainer on the cruise ships plying the Mediterranean, the Caribbean, and even more exotic locations had provided great shopping opportunities and I had stocked up with costumes and kaftans for both of us. Who would have thought that they would come in so useful this far in the future?

The more businesslike everyday outfits she had chosen for herself were about what I would have expected. Excellent materials, beautifully cut, but in muted colours, designed to be quiet and unobtrusive. Just what I would have chosen myself to dress the act. A good secretary doesn't outshine her employer's ladies. Not if she's wise.

No, nothing wrong with the costumes in themselves, except . . . I could feel my frown deepening. Something wasn't quite right. I walked into the closet for a closer inspection.

The light didn't work. I flipped the switch several times before looking up to discover that the bulb was missing. I settled for propping the door open with a stray shoe and looked around.

At first, nothing to cause disquiet was immediately apparent. Here and there a hanger hung askew, the garment half slipping off it, and there were uneven spaces between the hangers. Not like Nessa.

Then, as my eyes grew accustomed to the dim light, I noticed the sleeve of a jacket, half inside out, and the lining of a pocket protruding from another jacket.

Moving forward to investigate, I stumbled over a pile of

shoes in the middle of the floor. I recognized the mate to the one I had propped the door open with. The others were all jumbled together, instead of being lined up in matching pairs as Nessa usually kept them.

Had Nessa dressed hurriedly that last night, changing whatever she had been wearing for something more suitable for outdoors? And why had she gone out into the cold and darkness where relentless guard dogs patrolled the grounds? Had she been summoned? By whom? And why?

The whole set-up whispered of haste and urgency. But was it on Nessa's part – or was there another reason?

I stepped back into the bedroom, kicking the doorstop shoe into the pile with the others and letting the door close behind me.

One after the other, I pulled open the dressing-table drawers and looked down into them. Into the uneven heaps that had once been neat tidy piles of Nessa's underclothes and personal belongings. There was now no doubt about it: the place had been thoroughly, if amateurishly, searched.

And what about her desk? Surely that would have been a prime target. I turned towards the living room to see – in the cold light of day and the cold knowledge I had gained – just what I might have missed the night before.

I had forgotten the cat again. She sat beside the door opening into the cloister, staring at me accusingly.

'No, you can't go out,' I said. 'You heard those dogs last night. Some of them might still be around. I'm sure you're not an outside cat, anyway.' Nessa would never have allowed her precious pet to run loose in such dangerous territory. What a shame she hadn't taken the same precaution herself.

The cat flicked her ears irritably. I wasn't getting the message. She rose slowly and pointedly began to sniff along the bottom of the door.

Then I saw it. A small white triangle slipped beneath the door. I stooped and pulled it towards me cautiously.

Not a message from Beloved, I hoped, although I wouldn't put it past him. Even more cautiously, I opened the envelope – and relaxed.

Good morning, Vanessa.

I didn't want to wake you (Dr Anderson *emphasized* the importance of your getting plenty of rest), so you'll find brunch just outside.

We all hope you'll feel able to join us for dinner this evening. We gather in the library at 6:30 for 7:00.

If you need anything or have any questions, please contact me at H1 on your interior phone.

Monica

The cat was dancing with impatience while I read the message. Now that I thought of it, I was hungry. I checked my watch: 11:45. How time flies when you're having fun!

Holding the cat back with one foot, I eased the door open and looked up and down the cloister walk. It was deserted. An elaborate hostess trolley stood just outside the door. I tried to keep the cat away while I opened the door wide enough to roll the trolley inside.

I needn't have worried. She wasn't going anywhere. Not now that the trolley was on her side of the door. She hurled herself against my ankles, nearly tripping me and purring enthusiastically.

The truce was on again. At least until she had cajoled a goodly portion of my brunch away from me.

'I'm hungry, too,' I told her. 'But don't worry. There's enough in here for a regiment.'

A warming compartment held scrambled eggs, bacon, sausages and – in case they didn't appeal – kedgeree. Also an assortment of rolls and croissants.

A cool compartment beneath it had pots of yogurt, orange juice, small jugs of milk and cream, pats of butter, both salted and unsalted, and a variety of cheeses, all keeping nicely chilled.

The last panel revealed a neutral compartment holding a selection of fruit and Danish pastries.

'*Prryah-yah-yah!*' my new best friend enthused, pawing at the warming compartment. She couldn't wait.

'Oh, all right,' I surrendered. The warmed plates were in a wide lower drawer and I took two out, piling a bit of everything on hers and rather more of everything on mine, and we settled down to a long satisfying meal.

Old habits die hard – and why shouldn't they? When we had eaten our fill, I salvaged the remaining cheeses, butter, jams and a couple of rolls and folded them into a napkin and secreted them at the bottom of a drawer. In a place like this, you never could tell when you might get your next meal.

The cat watched with approval. She was indifferent to the rolls and jam, but she had a vested interest in those luscious cheeses.

'Just in case,' I told her.

She blinked agreement, just before she slumped across my feet and conked out, her little tummy bulging.

I wondered when she had last been fed – and how well. She had gulped down everything on offer, even the scrambled eggs, like some stray unsure of when – or what – her next meal would be.

But she had the right idea. I yawned. A little catnap right now was not to be despised. It was not just the heavy meal, it had been a pretty sleepless night. I vaguely recognized that I was also probably experiencing some sort of delayed shock after the last few days.

I gathered up the cat's unprotesting form and carried her into the bedroom where we both collapsed on to the bed and into those everloving arms of Morpheus.

Chapter Four

They were all so much older than I had thought. Beautifully nipped and tucked, Botoxed and liposuctioned, their smooth unlined faces turned towards me as I hesitated in the doorway. A faint golden glow about them might have been honey – or the amber they had been preserved in.

I looked around at them, my face as blank as theirs. Blanker, I was holding mine steady lest a passing flicker betray that they were not completely unknown to me. Decades of exposure in headlines, gossip columns, social notes and endless photographs had ensured that the public were aware of their names, faces and exploits.

But I had amnesia.

We held the tableau for a long moment then, abruptly, they all seemed to relax. Whatever they had expected – or feared – hadn't happened. On face after face, the tightly stretched lips forced themselves into welcoming smiles.

And yet, I was conscious of a wave of hostility eddying towards me from someone – or perhaps more than one. What had Nessa ever done to them – except be a generation or two younger? In these circles, that could be enough.

'Vanessa –' The first to speak was a painfully thin woman whose blonde hair was pulled back so tightly into a chignon that it constituted a facelift in itself. 'How good to have you back. And you look so . . . well . . .' Her voice trailed off uncertainly.

'Better than we expected, she means.' A larger woman

with improbably black hair translated. 'How are you feeling? Really?'

'Oh . . .' I waved a hand vaguely. 'A bit . . . disorientated, I'm afraid.' My smile was equally vague.

'Vanessa –' Monica Chandler stepped forward to place a reassuring hand on my shoulder. 'You'll soon remember everyone. Yvonne Beauclerc.' She indicated the blonde. 'And Candy Shaeffer.' The black-haired one. Her voice was carefully neutral. I couldn't tell whether she liked them or hated them.

They both nodded to me. Their lips stretched wider, revealing white shining teeth.

Oh, the shark has pretty teeth, dear . . . The melody of 'Mack the Knife' began to play at the back of my mind. I'd be willing to bet that both the dear ladies were as expert as he when it came to wielding knives.

The curious hush was back in the room. It was up to me to break it.

'How do you do,' I said politely. Again there was that sense of relaxation from somewhere. Or someone.

'Amanda Sloane.' Monica continued prompting, as another blonde clone nodded and raised her glass to me.

There was a faint movement at the back of the library and I saw two more slip out through a door I hadn't noticed. When it swung back into place, I saw why it wasn't noticeable. Shelves of books had been either built into it or painted on to it, so that it merged seamlessly into the other bookshelves. If I hadn't caught it in action, I'd never have known the door was there. I wondered how many other clever little tricks were scattered around the place. And whether the door led into another room – or a secret passage.

'Here you are –'

I jumped involuntarily. I hadn't been aware of anyone coming up on the other side of me. And that voice –

'– your usual.' He held a glass of amber liquid out to me, his eyes trying to meet mine with what was obviously intended to be a meaningful look.

And this was my Beloved? I didn't think so. Not unless Nessa had lost every shred of taste or sense that she had ever had.

It wasn't that he was overweight, pudgy was more like it. Nor that he was too tall and the over-solicitous way he bent towards me encroached on my space and made me uncomfortable. His moustache needed trimming and his fingernails were bitten to the quick.

I took the glass gingerly, managing to avoid the fingers trying to brush against mine as I did so. I also avoided meeting his eyes and the entreaty in them: that one side-long glance had been quite enough for me, thank you.

'Are you all right?' he queried earnestly. 'Really all right? I can't believe –'

'I told you, Ivor –' there was now a trace of asperity in Monica's tone – 'she doesn't remember a thing. Not what happened, not this place, not you, not me, not any of us.'

'But –' His look pleaded with me to deny it.

I gave a sad faint nod and took a sip of my drink, expecting Scotch. An involuntary shudder racked me and I set the drink down hastily on the nearest occasional table.

'You don't like it!' Ivor was stricken. 'But I made it just the way you always liked it.'

'Perhaps my tastes have changed,' I said faintly. The drink may have been Scotch-based, but it was over-powered by the amaretto that had been added. It was too sweet, cloying and faintly repulsive. Rather like Ivor himself, in fact.

'No!' Aghast, he appealed to Monica. 'Can that happen?'

'I don't see why not. I've heard of people losing their sense of smell or sense of taste after an accident.' She looked at me with concern. 'Have you –?'

'Oh, I can taste it,' I assured her. 'That's the trouble. It's much too sweet. Perhaps I could have just a plain Scotch?'

'Of course.' A brisk nod from Monica sent Ivor back to the drinks table.

'Better?' This time, he did not try to brush fingers, perhaps because everyone was watching.

'Much,' I approved. Whatever Nessa's tastes might have degenerated into, I was not prepared to go along with them. This was not the sort of establishment where one wished to ingest a heavy oversweet drink tasting so heavily of almonds that half a pint of cyanide could be masked by it.

'Perhaps you'll like it again –' Why was he so insistent? 'When you get your memory back.'

'Perhaps,' I said doubtfully.

'Nothing ever remains the same, Ivor.' Monica's firm hand on my shoulder propelled me gently forward and urged me down into an armchair. 'You should have learned that by now.'

His thin lips twisted, just before he raised his glass to cover them. His head dipped, then he turned his back on us to study the row of books on the shelf behind him. Sulking.

A movement in the doorway attracted everyone's attention. The air of expectation was palpable. Then he appeared and everyone deflated.

A tallish, darkish, saturnine young man in black denim jeans, black rollneck sweater, black shoes and socks, he might have stepped out of a Lowry painting. He looked over our heads to Monica. They stared at each other in wordless communication for a long moment, then he shook his head and disappeared.

As I raised my glass to my lips, I realized everyone else was doing the same. It was as fine an example of synchronized sipping as I had ever seen.

'It appears that Mr Oversall will not be joining us this evening,' Monica announced. 'Shall we go through to the dining room?'

'Where are Kiki and Nina?' Amanda looked around as she rose. 'I'm sure they were here a minute ago.'

'They slipped away some while ago.' So Monica had been paying closer attention than I had thought. 'I rather doubt that they'll be joining us.'

'Typical!' For such an elegant woman, Yvonne had a distinctly inelegant snort. 'Drink and run. And not even an apology.'

'Do they ever apologize?' Candy was realistic. 'They don't know the word exists.'

'A law unto themselves.' Ivor was conciliatory. 'As ever.'

Place settings were being removed as we entered the dining room and Monica, that guiding hand at my shoulder, moved to the head of the table and seated me at her right. On the other side of me was an exceptionally wide gap, the place setting still to be taken away.

Either these people weren't much given to conversation, or I was the skeleton at the feast, inhibiting them all. Hardly surprising when the odds were that someone here had planned for 'me' to be an actual skeleton by this time. I kept a determinedly pleasant expression on my face and resisted all attempts to draw me into conversation, not that there were that many. I also took the precaution of stifling an occasional yawn and drooping wearily from time to time.

Somewhere between the wild mushroom soup and the tournedos Rossini, someone glided into the place beside me. Since I was talking to – or rather, listening to – Monica at that moment, I couldn't turn, but was subliminally conscious that I hadn't heard the scrape of a chair.

'Good evening, Madame.' Monica looked beyond me, greeting the latecomer and freeing me to turn and look for myself.

The elderly woman in the wheelchair grunted some sort of acknowledgement, angling her head awkwardly in Monica's direction. You rarely see such bad cases of osteoporosis these days and, when you do, they're usually in the elderly, those whose earliest days were before the milk-and-orange-juice era that might have protected them. Her head was bent so far forward that her chin was brushing her collarbone and the steep hump in her back was almost level with the top of that bowed head.

I was glad that the wheelchair was pushed far enough beneath the table to hide her legs from view. I realized now that there had been no other chair waiting there, which was why I had assumed that the place setting was in the process of being cleared away.

'So?' There was nothing wrong with her brain. Her snapping black eyes raked me and I was thankful for the flickering candlelight and shadows. 'You are back. You are better?'

I nodded wordlessly, feeling that she had half-hypnotized me with that piercing gaze. I did not trust my voice.

'She's still quite fragile.' Monica answered for me. 'As I explained –'

'We are all fragile!' Madame cut her off sharply, then lost interest in anything else as the maid slid a bowl of the fragrant soup in front of her. She snatched up her spoon greedily and began catching up with the rest of us.

'A difficult day, Richie?' Monica murmured sympathetically to the man who had just taken the chair on the other side of her.

'No more than most.' He saw me looking at him and gave me a matter-of-fact nod. I began to like him, he was the first one who didn't treat me as some sort of freak show. I wondered if he was a particular friend of Nessa's.

The staff were well trained. As soon as she put down her spoon, Madame's empty bowl was whisked away and replaced with her tournedos. She gave a brief nod of satisfaction and attacked them. The rest of us had nearly finished, but she would catch up with us for dessert.

'We usually adjourn to the drawing room for coffee.' Monica draped her napkin beside her plate. Of course, no dessert. With this crew, anything sweet and calorie-laden would be out of the question. I should have known. I gave her a weak smile.

'Are you all right?' She looked at me with concern. 'Quite all right?'

'Actually . . .' I took the cue gratefully. 'I – I'm not really sure. I seem to be . . . fading out. If I might be excused . . .?'

'Of course.' She rose swiftly. 'I'll see you back to your quarters. I hope this hasn't been too much for you. You should have had a few days of rest before – And then meeting everyone all at once –' Her face creased with concern. 'I should have thought of that. Shall I call Dr Anderson? I hope he won't be angry with me.'

'No, no, I'm just a bit tired, that's all.' Everyone was watching me openly now, I had never had such an avid audience. In lieu of a bow, I swayed a little to give them that extra frisson.

'Here, let me.' Monica tried to take my arm. I'd over-done it.

'No, no, I'm fine.' I shrank away. *Look all you like, but mustn't touch!* The unwritten rule of all the clubs I had ever played in was firm in my mind. It applied more than ever here. And now.

'I'm sorry.' I apologized to the others with a gallant little smile. 'I'm afraid I'm not as strong as I thought I was . . .' I faltered to a stop as, in looking around, I inadvertently met Ivor's gaze. He was quivering with a sympathy and understanding I didn't believe for one instant. He also appeared to be trying to signal something to me.

'I need rest now,' I said firmly. 'Lots of rest. I'll take a sleeping pill, perhaps two . . .' That should be plain enough – even to him. The bolt on the door would rein-force the message.

'That sounds like an excellent plan.' Monica still hovered at my side, obviously prepared to catch me if I fainted. 'And you mustn't dream of trying to join us tomorrow evening if you don't feel completely up to it.'

We were out of the dining room now and walking along

the cloister. I dared to straighten up and walk a bit faster.

'Slow down,' Monica said. 'You're already too tired. You don't want to overdo it.'

'Yes . . . yes, you're right. I'm sorry . . .' I slowed, swayed and fluttered, going into my modified dying-swan routine again. 'But suddenly, I just . . . wanted to get back . . . to lie down . . . to sleep . . .'

'You *have* overdone it.' Monica was contrite. 'I should have insisted you stay quiet for a few days before you attempted anything social. It was too much for you.'

'It was just . . . all those people . . . all at once,' I apologized. 'And all of them strangers to me . . . and they didn't seem to know they were.'

'I understand,' Monica assured me. 'I'll speak to them again. And I'll see that you take it easier. I'll have your meals served in your room for the rest of the week. That should give you time to get your bearings.'

'No, please –' I'd overplayed it, the last thing I wanted was to be confined to quarters for days. 'I don't want to be any bother to you.'

'It's no bother for me.' Monica smiled faintly. 'If you had any memory, you'd know we keep a full staff. They'll take care of everything.'

'Of course. I should have known. Dinner was served so smoothly . . . so unobtrusively.'

'They either train up well,' Monica nodded in self-congratulation, 'or they don't last. Everett Oversall demands perfection – and pays for it.'

I had the uneasy feeling that I had just been given a not-particularly-coded message. Had Nessa not been shaping up satisfactorily? Or was there something else she might remember – if she could?

'Here we are.' With relief, I pulled the key from the pocket of my kaftan as we reached my door.

Monica's eyebrows flicked upwards, but she didn't comment. I gathered that no one locked their doors around here. But they didn't know what I knew.

'Goodnight.' I cut off any possible suggestion that she might accompany me any farther. 'And thank you.'

'Not at all.' She stepped back. 'I hope you sleep well.'

So did I. With a final exchange of smiles, I closed the door gently as she turned away. For a long moment, I leaned against the door, eyes closed, while the tension drained out of me. It had been harder than I had anticipated, but now that I had jumped the first hurdle, it might be easier.

I locked the door and shot the bolt home. Before I went to dinner, I had closed the inner shutters, drawn the heavy floor-length curtains and left a small lamp alight so that I wouldn't come back to darkness. Even so, there was something that did not feel right. I looked around uneasily.

Where was the cat?

'Gloriana?' I called. 'Glori –?'

No response. No sign of her.

I replayed the last few minutes in my mind. I hadn't opened the door wide, just enough to allow me to slip through. I had felt no movement at my feet, as of a cat darting out. When I had turned to close the door, Monica was the only one walking along the cloister. The cat couldn't have moved out of sight that quickly.

She must still be in here. Hiding.

'Glori –? It's only me. I thought we were friends now. Where are you?' Checking dark corners on the way, I moved into the bedroom. 'Come out, come out, wherever you are. Glori . . .?'

She *had* to be here. Somewhere.

'Gloriana? Duchess?'

I was conscious of a faint movement, a stirring where the bedspread brushed the floor.

Slowly, cautiously, a little pink nose poked out.

'It's all right. You can come out. You're safe.'

Why had I said that? Why shouldn't she be safe, here alone in Nessa's bedroom?

The rest of the head emerged, ears laid back, eyes

37

wild and frightened. Seeing no one but me, she came all the way out from under the bed, her fur bristled, her tail a bush.

'What the hell?' I stooped to pick her up. She cringed and stiffened in initial resistance, but as I cuddled her against my chest, she caught the scent of Nessa's perfume and stopped struggling.

'What's the matter? What's spooked you?'

She looked up at me and allowed herself one faint plaintive mew before turning her head away to stare anxiously around the room.

I followed her gaze, turning my head with hers, until it stopped at the closet door and her tiny body quivered. If she weren't a cat, she'd make a good bird dog. The door was ajar.

I was sure I had closed it. Nessa and I always closed doors. It was the way we had been brought up; you don't waste money by heating unused spaces.

'Have we had a visitor?' I murmured soothingly, creeping up on the door. 'An intruder? While I was out . . .?'

In the pool of sudden light when I swung the door open, I could see that the suitcase I had supposedly brought home from the hospital had been moved slightly. I bent to inspect it. The lock seemed a little scratched, but it had not been broken. I was glad that I had locked my make-up box safely inside.

Whatever someone was looking for, it seemed that they had not found it in the original search. Apparently, they had concluded that it had gone to hospital with me and they hoped I had brought it back.

Gloriana lifted her head suddenly and growled. But not at me. She was staring into the darkness at the back of the closet.

'All right.' I straightened up and could just barely discern a dark shape trying to blend into the shadows. 'I suggest you come out now. With your hands raised.' I put a lifetime of thriller-attending menace into the implied threat, although the worst I could shoot at anyone was an angry cat. That might have been enough.

'That sodding cat!' One of the blonde clones walked slowly forward. 'It gave me away, didn't it?'

Chapter Five

Gloriana stretched out her neck and hissed violently; the dislike was mutual.

'She's a clever girl.' I stroked Gloriana fondly. 'Unlike some I could mention. Who are you? How did you get in here? I locked the door when I went out to dinner and it was still locked just now.'

'That means nothing here.' She faced me defiantly. 'As you very well know.'

'No, I don't know. I don't know what you're talking about. I don't even know who you are.'

'You don't think I believe that!' But there was a trace of uncertainty in her voice.

'Believe it or not –' I shrugged – 'it's the truth.'

'I heard . . . we were told . . . about your . . . problem. But I can't believe you don't remember *me*. We're friends . . . best friends.' She moved forward and reached out to touch my arm. 'Confidantes.'

Gloriana hissed again. She stepped back quickly.

'Don't you believe me?'

Frankly, I preferred to believe the cat. Her opinion of the stranger seemed to be on a par with her opinion of Beloved – and she had been right about him.

'Vanessa –' she tried again. 'I must talk to you. Remind you –'

'So, in your anxiety to have a girlish chat, you sneak in here and hide in my closet?'

'That . . . that was a mistake.' She hung her head. 'I realized it as soon as I heard your key in the lock. That was why I changed my mind and hid in the closet. I was going to stay there until you were asleep, then leave and talk to you in the morning.'

'Mmm-hmmm. And you left the door ajar so that you could peek out and watch for the coast to be clear.' And wouldn't she have got an eyeful?

'I'd have been very quiet. You'd never have known.'

But you would. I looked at her, keeping my face blank. She was one of the two who had slipped out of the library, who had not appeared at dinner. Too busy taking the opportunity to search my rooms. I'd caught her, but where was her friend?

'Vanessa, don't look at me like that.' She stretched out her hand again, but Gloriana shifted in my arms and she pulled it back swiftly. 'I said I'm sorry. I apologize. I didn't mean to upset you. You're my friend –'

'I'm still waiting for you to tell me your name,' I said coldly.

'Kiki . . .' she faltered. 'Vanessa, it's *me*, Kiki.'

'Kiki *who?*'

'Kiki – Oh, God, I can't believe this! Kiki van Grooten.'

'Kiki van Grooten.' We were making progress. 'You're Dutch, then. Your English is very good.'

'No, oh, no!' She looked at me in horror. 'You *know* that's my stepfather's name. Mummy married Janwillem van Grooten, the diamond merchant. I'm as English as you are!'

'Be that as it may,' I said coldly, 'suppose you give me back my key.' I held out my hand.

'Oh, I can't believe this!' But she produced a key from some fold of her clothing and reluctantly held it out, keeping her distance from the cat. 'And we were such good friends,' she mourned.

'And we might be again.' Somehow, I didn't believe it for a moment. 'Once we have a chance to get re-acquainted.'

'I don't know.' She shook her head sadly. 'You . . . you seem changed. You're . . . harder . . . unforgiving.'

41

Getting pushed off a parapet will do that to a girl. And that was an interesting word for her to use. What else was there to forgive? More than just snooping around in my quarters, I suspected.

'Perhaps the fall brought out another side of my personality.' I whisked the key away from her. 'And if anyone else has any of these, you might pass the word that I want them back. Or perhaps it might be simpler to have the lock changed.'

'If you think that will make any difference –' for a moment, her mask of contrition slipped and she was openly, blatantly mocking – 'then you really *have* lost your memory!'

'Well,' I said to the Duchess as the door slammed behind our unwanted visitor, 'what was that all about? And are there any more around like her?'

Evidently not. Relaxed now, the cat abandoned my protective arms and leaped to the floor, heading for the shelf that held the cat crunchies. Repelling invaders can bring on an appetite.

I gave her a generous handful – she'd earned them – and went back to investigate the farthest reaches of that closet to make certain that no one else was lurking there. Like her friend, Nina, for instance – they had left the library together.

But, wherever she was, Nina wasn't in there. What was? I wondered. What was it they were looking for? Something small, since, having once searched the place, they were trying again, with particular attention to the suitcase I had brought back from the hospital. The most valuable – and incriminating – thing in that was my make-up box. The real reason I kept any case containing it locked at all times. Engagements at too many slippery little clubs on the way up had taught me that helping themselves to other people's make-up was one of the things certain performers could be conscienceless about. Rather like not returning books, I suppose. Some things were deemed to be public property – unless you kept a good watch on them.

Somewhere outside, a seagull called again – or perhaps another cat. Gloriana cocked her head to listen.

'Friend of yours?' I asked.

She gave me her huffy Duchess look. It was obviously none of my business.

'Only asking.' I shrugged and turned away. I could be indifferent, too.

The cry outside was not repeated; the silence deepened. I wondered what the others did through the long nights. Unless they all had small television sets secreted in their rooms. Officially, television was barred, Nessa had told me in one of her early letters, except for the cinema-size set in the study. Old Oversall liked to keep his companions around him in his leisure hours – and he chose the programmes for viewing himself. It wouldn't be surprising if there were a few smuggled sets around. Most of the ladies comprising his retinue had been independent spirits with minds of their own – until he had suborned them.

Perhaps the younger ones still were. And perhaps it didn't matter so much any more to the older ones; their world had faded away, as all worlds do. No more the glitzy nightclubs where they had sipped champagne from crystal glasses while music with melodies and narrative lyrics played softly in the background.

The sort of places where Yvonne Beauclerc had started her career, sighing, gurgling and moaning her laments of lost love and betrayal into the blue haze of cigarette smoke that helped create the cloudy dreamy sense of unreality and a private world only found in old movies these days.

Which was where Yvonne had had a few more brief moments of fame. But, as was usual when film makers found themselves with a chanteuse under contract, they didn't know what to do with her. A few appearances as a featured player – always in nightclub scenes, crooning into a microphone while the camera cut away to the more important business of the hero and heroine at a nearby table, invariably plotting together to uncover a killer, or a spy ring, and falling in love.

After a few of these clinkers, Yvonne had returned to the international cabaret circuit, trading on her screen credits as much as her voice.

Somewhere along the way, Everett Oversall had entered the scene and she had become his 'new romance', as the gossip columnists of the day – ever careful of the libel laws – had tactfully phrased it.

Oh, yes, I'd done my homework on the Internet before I came here, pulling up everything possible on Oversall's background. Most of it was from files of tabloid newspaper gossip from his playboy years; he had kept an exceptionally low profile before that.

But the meeting with Yvonne had been the beginning of his nightclubbing phase. Constant photographs had appeared in all the tabloids and some of the broadsheets. It became noticeable that his entourage was expanding. He collected Candy Shaeffer in New York and added Amanda Sloane in London. While others came and went, they remained to form a stable core.

A few years later, when Oversall shares wobbled a bit and shareholders grew restless, most of the publicity ceased. The earlier, more serious and work-centred Oversall re-emerged; a man dedicated solely to his business interests. All mention of the women in his background disappeared, although they didn't.

Rumour had it that Candy Shaeffer, who had cut her fangs as a New York public relations executive, was masterminding the repositioning of Oversall in the business world. It worked. There hadn't been a photograph of him in anything but Captain of Industry mode for the last decade or so.

Amazing how much one can gather from the gossip columns over the years. Now all I had to do was keep pretending that I didn't know a thing and couldn't recognize anyone from anywhere.

'Tricky,' I told my audience. 'Very tricky.'

The cat had been crouched nearby, watching closely as I went through my bedtime routine. She blinked when I finished shaving and rubbed in moisturizer.

Nessa's moisturizer, smooth and creamy, with a faint scent of lilacs, bringing back the springtimes of our childhood, when the lilac bushes in the garden came into full bloom and their heavy fragrance blended with the sea air. I wondered if that were why Nessa used this particular brand; it would remind her, too, of those carefree days.

Nessa! My heart twisted abruptly. How was she now? Why had there been no news? Because there was none or . . .

Or because *I* was Nessa now. Dr Anderson could not issue bulletins on the state of a patient presumably discharged and back in circulation. I would get a private report when he came to examine 'me' and check 'my' progress.

Eyes wide, whiskers quivering, the cat inched forward a bit. I could see her problem: I looked like Vanessa, I smelled like Vanessa, but . . .

Suddenly she straightened up, alert and turning towards the outer door. I followed her into the sitting room and up to the door.

Nothing to be seen, nothing to be heard, the doorknob wasn't moving. But I trusted my little honorary bird dog – and she was pointing.

We both waited silently. Nothing happened. Perhaps the cat was just as jumpy as I was right now and it was a false alarm. Or someone had passed by, walking innocently along the cloister.

Then she moved forward again, neck stretched out, nose twitching. I saw that something had already happened.

A triangular corner of paper almost the same shade as the carpet peeked from beneath the door. We both eyed it mistrustfully.

I decided I was in no hurry to pick it up. The cat looked up at me impatiently, but I shook my head.

'Later,' I whispered. If anyone was lurking about out-side, waiting for me to discover their missive, let them wait until they gave up and went away.

I chose a book from Nessa's shelves and tried to read. The cat continued to stand guard at the door.

After half an hour, I joined her to slowly pull in our catch and examine it. It was a small plain card, the size of a calling card.

The message was printed in block capitals:

WHEN YOU REMEMBER,
I'LL BE WAITING.

I stared at it for a long time, wondering which way to read it.

As a romantic promise? Or a threat?

Chapter Six

The Duchess alerted me in the morning, jumping on the bed and ramming her cold wet nose into my ear just as the breakfast trolley was trundling into the cloister. I barely had time to jam on my turban and swirl my kaftan over me before opening the door to it.

'Oh!' Round eyes widened in a round little face staring up at me from atop a round little body. 'I expected you to be still asleep. I was going to leave it outside the door.'

'Not this morning.' I smiled down at her reassuringly, almost as startled as she. Her presence reminded me that there was a whole sub-stratum of servants I had not yet encountered.

'Oh, Miss Nessa!' Recovering herself, she wheeled the trolley into the room. 'I'm so glad you're all right! We all are.'

'Thank you . . .' I hesitated. 'But you're going to have to help me out, I'm afraid I don't remember your name.'

'I'm Dilys, Miss Nessa.' Her eyes welled with tears. 'I'm sorry, I should have said. Miss Monica told us –'

'Yes, yes, all right.' I gave her another reassuring smile. I didn't want her blubbing all over me.

'You looked so awful when they took you away,' she wailed softly. 'I was so afraid. We were all afraid –'

'Thank you, Dilys, but I'm all right now.' I heard my voice waver. Was I? How *was* Nessa this morning? 'Except for my memory, that is.'

'If I can help,' she volunteered. 'If you want to ask me anything, anything at all –'

'Thank you, Dilys.' I mentally filed that offer for possible future use. 'I may take you up on that. When I can think of something I need to know.' I edged her back towards the door. 'And please thank everyone for their good wishes.'

'My number is 23 on the house phone.' She backed out slowly. 'Just ring if you want anything.'

'Thank you, Dilys, thank you so much.' With a final smile, I closed the door behind her and let my face relax.

Gloriana looked from me to the trolley and back again expectantly.

'Yes, thank you, too. Good work!' I praised her. Perhaps she had only been anxious to get her share of breakfast, but I was glad to have been alerted to its arrival. I no longer felt comfortable with the thought of the trolley being left to stand outside my door for any length of time. Food could be too easily tampered with.

We settled down to our meal and I rewarded her with a kipper and most of the coffee cream, of which she was duly appreciative.

We might not quite trust each other, but we were settling down into being a team.

By mid-morning, I was feeling too restless to remain confined to quarters. Besides, it looked like a good day outside. For November, that is. Although overcast, it wasn't actually raining – and an invalid ought to take a bit of fresh air, oughtn't she? A turn around the grounds – the immediate grounds, obviously; the estate was too huge to be encompassed in a single stroll – might not go amiss.

A voluminous navy blue pashmina shawl hung from a hook just inside the closet. It seemed more suitable than either of the coats or the cashmere blazer. I shook it out and wrapped it over my kaftan. Then, feeling rather like a Victorian waif, I stepped into the cloister and locked the door behind me.

Had Nessa felt the same when she wore this shawl? Of

course she had. Our tastes, thoughts and feelings were almost identical.

Almost . . . aye, there's the rub. There had been people over whom our opinions had diverged. Nessa was – *is, is.* She's not in the past tense yet. Not now, not ever! Nessa *is* more easy-going than I. She might not suffer fools gladly, but she suffers them. I'm more impatient, perhaps too impatient.

Surely, she would never have been as close to Ivor as he kept trying to insist. Beloved – like hell!

I was less sure about Kiki. She and her friend – if friends they were, nothing seemed certain around this place – had obviously joined Oversall's retinue after his retreat from the public scene, thus escaping the full glare of publicity. They were younger than the others, although still older than Nessa, but it was possible that one or both of them had been her friends.

It was also possible that they hadn't. What sort of friend goes searching through a mate's belongings in their absence? And what were they searching for? What had Nessa got herself into?

Somewhere in the distance, the plaintive cry of a seagull, or perhaps a stray cat, caught my attention. Could it really be a seagull? It seemed to come from ground level.

I followed the cries through a rose garden where many bushes still bore blooms thanks to the mild English climate. In most places, they wouldn't have stood a chance once winter was so near; here, there were still buds forming.

A wide flagstone-paved path lay, rather curiously, on the other side of the garden, stretching as far as I could see. Beyond it, a greensward sloped gently down to an ornamental lake dotted with waterlilies. Another stretch of lawn and then a grove of birch trees gleamed white against the pine forest behind them.

Not quite Capability Brown, but not bad. Not bad at all.

As I stood there, two brown hens scuttled out from the holly hedge bordering the path. A moment later, they were followed by a larger oddly shaped bird who appeared to be dragging a pile of brushwood behind him. One of them uttered another of those plaintive haunting cries.

The burdened bird stalked into the middle of the flag-stoned path and swung about to face me challengingly. I had the eerie feeling that he had recognized me as another male and was ready to fight to protect his females.

He stared directly at me then, with a surge of effort and a faint rattling noise, the pile of brushwood rose up behind his head and fanned out into a shimmering display of gloriously improbable colour. A peacock in his full glory, he faced me proudly.

'Fantastic!' I applauded enviously. What wouldn't I give for a stage costume half so magnificent. That iridescent green, with the deep royal blue, surrounded by burnished gold, of the spectacular eye that tipped each feather, the –

'Popinjay!' The harsh croak from behind made me jump. 'Just like all males. Popinjays – every one!'

Turning cautiously, at first I saw no one until I lowered my gaze to wheelchair level. She was glaring up at me, as though daring me to contradict her.

'Good morning, Madame.' It was safe to acknowledge her, wasn't it? After all, we had met last night.

'Come in here!' She wheeled back her chair and I realized why the path had been paved instead of gravelled. For her convenience.

'Yes, Madame.' I followed her through an opening in the hedge large enough to accommodate her chair and found myself in a raised garden. Greenery sprouted in profusion from deep earth-filled boxes mounted on trestle tables at wheelchair height. I recognized basil, rosemary, parsley and chives. I could smell sage and other familiar fra-grances. A herb garden, then, especially arranged for Madame, although I doubted that she did much gardening herself these days.

What Madame had done in the past was open to ques-tion. Rumours abounded: claims that she was the financial genius behind Oversall's empire; that she was his first mistress, who knew too much about his early shady deals – and had proof hidden away somewhere, so that he was afraid to drop her. There was even a faction that claimed she was his mother.

Whoever she was, she was here to stay. Till death did them part. And that was another story one heard: that, although much older, she had been his first wife – and still held the marriage certificate that would prove all his subsequent alliances were bigamous.

A mystery woman, indeed. Of indeterminate antiquity, unknown origins, vaguely foreign accent – and a determined grip on life. And on Everett Oversall.

Madame was still a force very much to be reckoned with.

'So!' She halted the chair abruptly and whirled it round to face me, with something of the same challenge the peacock had shown. 'You are recovered, eh?'

'Partly . . .' I said hesitantly.

'Ah, yes. The amnesia.' Her tone said she didn't believe a word of that story. 'How convenient. And clever . . . very clever.'

'But true.' I gave her a rueful smile, wondering what degree of intimacy she would proceed to claim.

'And you recall nothing?' She tipped her head back as far as it would go, her shrewd eyes assessing me.

'I can read and write.' I made a brave show of it. 'And use the right fork. All the automatic motor responses are in place. It's just the people who have slipped out of gear. And events, of course.'

'Vanessa!' She gave a small splutter of what might have been mirth in someone else. It was drowned out by the peacock's strident cry from the other side of the hedge.

Instinctively, I turned towards the sound in time to see a slight blonde figure dart through the opening into the herb garden.

'Nina!' Madame went white with fury. 'You have been told to leave those peacocks alone!'

'I didn't do it!' Too late, Nina tried to hide the glittering peacock feather behind her back. 'I was just looking at Percy, admiring him – and he knew it. He sort of shook himself and dropped the feather right at my feet. He *wanted* me to have it!'

Oh, yes? That story didn't quite jibe with the outraged cry we had heard from Percy. As was becoming usual around this place, I found that I believed the fauna more than the humans. No surprise there.

'Ah, yes?' Madame was equally sceptical.

'Anything the matter?' Unseen, unheard, the man called Richie had appeared and was hovering protectively over Madame.

'Nina is up to her tricks again,' Madame complained.

'I'm not!' Nina defended hotly. 'I don't have any tricks. I'm an artist! An interior designer. Right now, I'm in my Art Nouveau phase. I'm going to have a tall blue vase filled with peacock feathers in one corner of my studio – just like the Victorians used to do.'

'Forget that,' Richie said flatly. 'And stay away from the peacocks, Nina. You don't want Mr Oversall to lose patience with you.'

'He won't!' She sounded very sure of herself. 'He understands. He appreciates talent. He's going to set me up in my own design business in the West End in London soon.'

'Mmm-hmmm . . .' Richie had the bored expression of one who had heard that before. Perhaps often – and from a variety of 'talents'. 'Just leave the peacocks alone, see?'

'I suppose I can pick up any feathers I find around the grounds? They drop off all over the place. No one else wants them – and my vase is almost full.'

Madame snorted. Nina swung to face her and seemed to suddenly discover that I was there.

'Vanessa!' Almost visibly, you could see her deciding to use me to change the subject. 'I didn't notice you – I mean, I'm so glad to see you. You're looking –' She broke off in confusion.

'I'm sorry.' I smiled wanly, trusting to my pale foundation and even paler face powder to speak of my condition. 'I . . . I'm afraid I don't . . . That is, I met the others at dinner last night. I didn't see you.'

'I wasn't there. Inspiration called!' She gave a virtuous sniff. 'I was working in my studio.'

'Vanessa –' Madame picked up her cue. 'This is Nina Santana.' Her dry tone spoke eloquently of what she thought of that name. 'She is our . . . resident artist. Everett always likes to have one or two around. Nina, you already know Vanessa.'

'Of course I do.' Nina spoke warmly. 'Vanessa understands, too. She's going to let me redecorate her quarters so that they truly reflect her personality.'

Is she, indeed? I smiled vaguely. Another one staking her claim to a portion of Nessa's life.

'Now that you're back, we can get started. I wanted to do it while you were away, so that it would be a wonderful surprise for you. But –' she pouted – 'they wouldn't let me.'

Well, good for them. Nessa's quarters looked perfectly all right to me just the way they were – and I'm sure Nessa thought so, too.

'Monica said it would have to wait until you returned. Now we can go ahead,' she beamed.

'Well, perhaps not right away,' I said. 'I don't think I'm quite strong enough yet to face any disruption.'

'Of course she isn't!' Madame snapped.

'Have some sense, Nina,' Richie said. 'She needs peace and quiet for a while, not someone prancing around underfoot, changing everything.'

'Some *stranger*,' Madame underlined with a touch of malice. 'Poor Vanessa doesn't know you. She certainly won't know what your work is like.'

'I don't.' I didn't bother with the apologetic smile. Nina was beginning to get on my nerves.

'Oh, but you must come over to my studio! I'll show you what I'm doing. You loved it before –'

Won't you walk into my parlour? I'd rather not.

53

'Not right now.' I pulled my shawl more tightly around me and gave a visible shudder. 'I'm getting chilled, I'm afraid. I think I ought to go and lie down.'

'An excellent idea.' Madame, too, was fading fast. It had obviously been a strain to keep her head so high, now it lowered slowly and inexorably.

'I'll take you inside.' Richie moved forward quickly.

'Not yet!' Madame pushed his hands away. 'See to Nina first. Escort her safely back to her studio.'

'Oh, I'm perfectly safe,' Nina assured her blithely.

'It is not *your* safety I care about!' Madame snapped. 'It is Percy's. Do not let her near the peacocks.'

'Right, Madame.' Richie grasped Nina's arm firmly and led her away.

'Vanessa –' Madame hissed as her head slumped still further to rest her chin on her collarbone.

I had to lean close to hear her.

'Vanessa, you fool! Why did you come back?'

Chapter Seven

'No change,' Dr Anderson reported tersely. 'She's no better.'

'But no worse?'

The flick of his eyebrow told me that the only worse left was – I refused to think of that.

'She's holding her own?' I urged.

'Such as it is.' He shrugged uncomfortably. I still made him uneasy. The similarity – and the contrast – between the two 'Nessas' he was attending was almost more than he could cope with. I wondered how long he had been qualified and if this was his first post. If so, what a hornets' nest he had been thrown into.

'I think –' he glanced at his watch – 'I've spent a convincing length of time here now. I'd best be off on the rest of my rounds.'

'Rounds?'

'Oh, yes. I have some real patients, you know. Madame –' He shook his head and sighed.

'And Oversall himself?' I guessed.

'Not quite as sprightly as he used to be,' Anderson admitted. 'Doesn't do any harm to keep a quiet check on him.'

'Any others?'

'Oh . . .' He didn't like the question. Any moment now, he was going to invoke medical ethics. 'An ache here, a shooting pain there, a bit of general malaise. They're all getting on, you know, even if they'd rather die before they admitted it.'

But it was Nessa, the youngest of them all, who had come so close to death. Who might still –

'*Ooof!*' Gloriana, who had been strolling around the sitting room, had suddenly leaped into his lap, landing badly.

'Here –' He lifted her up and resettled her. 'That's better, but you can't stay, you know. I'm on my way.'

She responded by lifting her head so that he could stroke her throat. *Thank you, Gloriana.* That tells me he isn't a stranger to you, you know him and trust him. He's an accustomed visitor, probably dropping in for a cup of coffee and a chat with someone his own age after doing his rounds and treating the waxworks.

'That's enough.' He lowered her gently to the floor, undisturbed by the huffy Duchess look she gave him as she stalked away. I was glad to see I wasn't the only one she could deepfreeze. Anderson continued on his way to the door.

'When will I see you again?' The innocent question stopped him dead in his tracks.

He swerved around to face me with a look that combined disbelief, panic . . . and revulsion.

Was it because the question had sounded too feminine – or had I? Perhaps he had heard it too often from some ex-girlfriend. Or even from Nessa. And here was I, so much like her – yet not her.

'Look –' I dropped out of character, deepening my voice – 'you're my only contact, the only source of information about my sister, my twin. *That's* the only reason I give a damn about ever seeing you again!'

'Yes, yes, of course. Sorry.' He was struggling – whether to understand or to overcome his momentary revulsion, I couldn't tell. 'I – I try to call two days a week. Madame . . .' He let the explanation trail off. 'This is Tuesday. I'll probably call again on Friday. Unless there's an emergency.'

I nodded. Having seen Madame, I understood. She was the embodiment of the expression 'on borrowed time'.

'Oh, and . . .' Hand on doorknob, he paused. 'Perhaps I should warn you. I'd watch my step with Nina and Kiki, if I were you. They can be a bit . . . erratic.'

I nodded again. *Tell me something I don't know.*

And I wasn't going to huddle together and swap girlish secrets with any of the others, either.

'Are you okay now? Are you really okay? Honestly?' Candy Shaeffer had cornered me as I headed for the library and the preprandial drinks.

'Well, mostly,' I said demurely. 'Except for . . . um . . . the amnesia . . .'

'Oh, that!' Her flick of the wrist dismissed the problem as something less than an attack of hay fever. 'Memory is greatly overrated. After all, don't we reinvent ourselves periodically as we move along?'

Maybe you do in Public Relations, but most people take their lives more seriously. I shrugged and produced another of my wan non-committal smiles.

'You always agreed with me.' Here it came again, that insistence on an intimacy that might or might not have existed. 'We thought alike in so many ways – but there's something different about you now.' She eyed me thoughtfully. 'I wonder how much all this has changed you.'

'I wouldn't know.' I gave her a rueful smile this time. 'If I can't remember what I was like before, how can I know how much I've changed?'

'I envy you,' she said. 'Here you are: young, pretty, bright, with the future before you and no past. You're like a blank page.'

That's right. And everybody was queuing up to scribble all over me. I waited for her contribution.

'You know –' Sure enough, it came. 'I could do a lot with you.' Her eyes narrowed assessingly. 'I never did think you made enough of yourself. That mousy hair, those fade-into-the-background clothes, no make-up. You just weren't trying!'

Interesting – and confirming my own impression. Nessa knew as much about costume and make-up as anyone in the business. As children, our favourite games had involved the dressing-up box and the tray of discarded lipsticks, eyeshadows and liners and all the other bits and pieces of make-up we had scrounged from older relatives and friends.

There was even a time when Nessa's ambition had been to design costumes and stage settings. She had got off to a good start and then something had happened. A broken romance, I assumed, although I was on the other side of the world by then, so we couldn't discuss things as we used to. Not that Nessa had shown any sign of wanting to talk about it.

But something had daunted – if not quite broken – her spirit and the next thing I heard, she had taken this secretarial job with Overall. Licking her wounds? Skulking in her tent? Whatever, she had retreated from the world as she knew it – and found herself in a far more dangerous one. No wonder she had tried to fade into the background.

'Vanessa!' A hand was weaving back and forth in front of my face. 'Are you there?' Candy's voice was sharp, annoyed. 'Are you listening?'

'Sorry . . .' I swayed gracefully. 'I . . . I'm not used to standing for so long . . .'

'No, I'm sorry.' But there was no contrition in her voice. 'I should have realized that. Let's go and have a drink. You'll feel better.'

'Tell me,' I said, as we headed for the library. 'Were we close friends?'

'No.' She surprised me, the first not to claim to have been my bestest closest buddy. The first honest answer I had heard around this place.

'No, we weren't . . . then.' She turned and smiled, the

tips of her sharp white teeth gleaming below the painted curve of her lips. *Oh, the shark has pretty teeth, dear* . . .

'Not then. But we can be . . . now.'

'Here they are,' Monica said. 'We'd nearly given you up. I was afraid we'd overtired you yesterday.'

'Have a drink.' Ivor started forward, a glass in his hand.

'Thank you, I'd love a sherry.'

'But –' He stopped short, looking down at the glass. 'But you had Scotch yesterday,' he spluttered indignantly. 'I've got it all ready for you.'

I noticed that – which was why I'd opted for sherry. A girl can't be too careful these days. Not with drugs like Rohypnol and types like Ivor floating around.

'Tonight I'd prefer sherry,' I said firmly. The sherry bottle was full and still sealed.

'But –'

'For heaven's sake, Ivor, give her what she wants,' Monica said impatiently. 'A person doesn't have to have the same thing every night.'

'I'll have a sherry, too, for a change,' Candy chimed in, giving me a conspiratorial look which was not lost on Ivor. 'I think it's a mistake for people to get too set in their ways.'

'All right! All right!' Quietly fuming, Ivor went back to the drinks table, slammed down the unwanted Scotch and began making far too much clatter as he rummaged around for the knife to cut the seal on the sherry bottle. Having done that, he pulled out the sherry glasses with unnecessary force.

'Don't chip those glasses, Ivor,' Monica warned. 'Mr Oversall chose them himself in Venice years ago. It would be hard to replace them.'

'All right!' Pettishly, he splashed sherry into the fragile glasses and sulked when Candy stepped forward to take both of them and bring mine to me. Whatever he had planned – whether a suggestive brush of the fingers, or something more sinister with the Scotch – his wheel had been well and truly spoked.

I had taken a small armchair, bypassing a sofa with room for three. That didn't please Ivor, either.

Ignoring him, I sipped my sherry demurely and looked around at my new best friends.

They were all here. Even Kiki and Nina had deigned to join us and were smiling hopefully at me.

I counted the house again and realized that only Amanda Sloane and Yvonne Beauclerc had failed to approach me. They sat together, talking quietly. I wondered what their game was.

I had a clear view when the door opened and the black-clad figure leaned into the room. As before, he met Monica's eyes over our heads and signalled: *No*.

She nodded resignedly. She seemed to have expected nothing else.

Then, in the split second before he withdrew, I became aware that he was looking at me intently.

I glanced away, acting as though I hadn't noticed, but I felt the shuddering chill you're supposed to feel when someone walks over your grave. He hated me – and I didn't know why.

What had I – what had Nessa ever done to him? Was he someone she had picked up and then abandoned on the rebound from her unhappy love affair?

He was a more likely candidate than Ivor: younger, better looking –

'Shall we go in to dinner now?' Monica rose, making the question rhetorical. 'Mr Oversall won't be joining us this evening.'

Neither would Madame. The wheelchair-sized gap beside me remained unfilled, the table setting undisturbed.

Perhaps the day had been too much for her. The argument with Nina, the warning to me and then Dr Anderson's visit must have taken a lot out of her. She wasn't as strong as she used to be. I remembered the doctor's sigh and knew it might be more than that. She needed her rest.

Yet I felt cheated. I had hoped, under the cover of light table chat, to find something about what was going on around here. Her sudden outburst had told me that she believed Vanessa was in danger; her rudeness told me that she was probably more of a friend to Nessa than any of the other claimants sweet-talking themselves forward.

A throat was cleared quietly but emphatically. Not for the first time. Ivor was trying to catch my eye. He'd be lucky!

'Is Madame unwell?' I turned to Monica.

'Overtired, I'm afraid.' Monica frowned slightly. 'She tries to do too much. She doesn't like to admit she isn't as young as she used to be.'

'None of us are,' Yvonne said. Her candour earned her several poisonous glances.

'On the contrary, dear lady.' Ivor sent her such a melting smile that I wondered if she were another of his Beloveds. 'It is my strong impression that you grow younger looking and more beautiful every day.'

'*And she well may pass for forty-three . . . In the dark with a light behind her . . .*' Amanda Sloane trilled Gilbert and Sullivan maliciously.

'Ah, yes.' Yvonne slanted a look worthy of Madame at her. 'You, of course, are a connoisseur of passes!'

Hmmm . . . perhaps not such friends, after all. Of course, it was not necessary for allies to be friends. Mutual interests were enough to keep them together for the duration of the pact. But what pact?

'Perhaps –' Ivor cleared his throat again – 'one of you experts would be kind enough to *pass* the butter.' He glanced around the table with a roguish simper to make sure that we had all appreciated his wit.

What was it Dorothy Parker had said when challenged to a battle of wits? Something along the lines of, 'I refuse to fight an unarmed opponent.'

Everyone ignored him. He didn't even get the butter and had to reach for it himself.

After that, a glacial silence descended that lasted until the end of the meal.

I was not the only one to decline adjourning for coffee, although I was the only one with a ready-made excuse. The others simply darted away abruptly as they finished. I had to move fast to avoid being left alone at the table with Beloved.

Monica hesitated in the doorway behind me, effectively blocking Ivor's attempted pursuit. Was it just a fortuitous happening, or did she derive some satisfaction of her own from foiling his intentions?

I didn't linger to hear what she had to say to him, but made my way steadily to my own quarters. I wanted to be in them with the door securely bolted before Ivor got away from Monica.

As I turned the corner into the cloister, something stirred at the far end. A dark shape emerged from the shadows and glided slowly towards the anchorite's cell.

A monk? Or the ghost of one? What I could see of the long flowing robes, lightly cinched at what might have been a waist, the bowed head, the processional pace, all gave that impression.

Then the figure stopped, half-turned and, with a vague gesture, seemed to be inviting me to follow him.

Chapter Eight

Was that what Nessa had done? Had seen? Had followed out of the cloister, through the adjoining buildings, to the tower and the parapet from which she had fallen?

Ahead of me, the figure turned again and raised its arm in a more imperious gesture, commanding my presence.

Not bloody likely! No, thank you, Brother, Father, Whoever – Whatever – you are. Not this lady. Whatever your game is, I'm not playing.

I had the key in my hand as I reached my door. I inserted it and turned it quickly in the lock, slipping inside without a backward glance.

The sitting room was warm and welcoming after the icy cold of the cloister. They say the presence of a ghost is marked by a distinct drop in the temperature. On the other hand, a dank chill is not unknown on a late November evening.

The apparition also posed an interesting question about psychic technicalities: would the genuine ghost of a medieval monk haunt premises that were a Victorian fake? Or was it the spirit of the suicidal butler who had departed in the purloined costume of the monk?

The cat was curled up in a corner of the sofa, comfortable and unconcerned. If the paranormal had passed by, it hadn't intruded on her consciousness.

'So, nobody here but us chickens, eh?' I asked her.

She deigned to open one eye and close it again.

Nobody. I made a mental note to add near-sightedness

and blurred vision to my list of traumas, just in case the 'monk' was someone I had met who was playing games.

But which one of them? The only person who might be stupid enough to pull such a trick was Ivor. Did he imagine that, if he showed up after giving 'Nessa' a good fright, she would fall into his arms thinking he was a rescuer? Only, he had not had time enough to get away from Monica, race to the far end of the cloister and change into costume before I arrived to catch his act.

Then who? And why? The only certainty was that there was someone in the house deeply chagrined at the failure of his plot to . . . to what? Entrap me? Dispose of me?

Time would tell. But how much time did I have? The spectral appearance could mean that someone was growing nervous and anxious to finish me – Nessa – off. This attempt had fallen flat, but what other tricks did he have up his flowing sleeves?

Dilys was tight-lipped and unwilling to linger when I took the breakfast tray from her in the morning.

'Sorry, Miss Vanessa,' she said, 'can't stop. Bit of a flap on. Got to get straight back, they're waiting for me. Miss Monica says for you to rest today. I'll bring you your lunch later.' She hurried off before I could ask her any questions.

'Now what?' I asked the cat instead.

She didn't know and couldn't have cared less, her entire attention was centred on the tray in my hands.

When I set it down and lifted the lid, I found the main attraction was scrambled eggs with smoked salmon. An urgent mew and furry body twined around my ankles told me that would do nicely.

My temporary best friend and I enjoyed the breakfast, then she returned to aloofness and sauntered off to nap until the next meal.

At the sound of an approaching motor, I drew back the inside shutters on the window facing the outer world and stood behind the curtains to watch Dr Anderson's car roar into view.

Nessa! I hurried out and intercepted him before he could reach the front door. He was carrying the traditional black bag.

'Not now, Nessa!' he said impatiently. 'This is more import –' He broke off, glaring at me accusingly.

'God! the tricks the mind can play!' he exploded. 'Even knowing what I know, for one second, I actually thought you –'

'Don't say it,' I warned.

'No, no. I wasn't going to.' He became abstracted, but brusque. 'However the message is still the same . . . Vanessa. Go back to your quarters and stay there. This has nothing to do with . . . you.'

'Madame?' My heart sank. Had I lost my chance to find out what she knew?

'No, no! She may not look it, but she's in better shape than some of them.'

'Then who? Oversall?'

'He'll outlive us all.'

'But –'

'Just go inside and keep out from underfoot!' He gave me a sardonic grimace. 'It's nothing for you to bother your pretty little head about!'

I slammed the door behind me then kicked the waste-paper basket across the room and, for good measure, followed it with a few books.

The cat narrowed her eyes at me and prudently retreated beneath the bed. She wasn't going to get underfoot, either.

Pretty little head – hell! It was a low blow – and a deliberate one.

As though, somewhere in that tricky mind of his, Anderson was blaming me – hating me – for not being Nessa.

Monica had sent a message suggesting that I rest today. Dr

Anderson had told me bluntly to keep out of the way. What was going on?

Deciding that a short stroll through the gardens could pass as heeding the spirit, if not the letter, of the barely concealed orders, I draped the shawl around my kaftan and stepped outside.

In a slow pace suitable to an invalid, I walked the length of the cloister to the cell at the end. Nothing had changed there: the wax anchorite in monk's robes still knelt in position, head bowed, face concealed.

What had I expected? An empty cell? A changed position? A sudden rising to the feet and another imperious gesture to follow him – or her? It was just a waxwork. Everett Oversall picking up and continuing the nasty joke of the original owner of Friary Keep. Well, Oversall had never been renowned for his sense of humour.

With a curious reluctance to turn my back on the figure, I moved out on to the lawn beyond the cloister. It was deserted. No sign of life anywhere. Not even a peacock. I might have been a ghost myself, victim of a time-slip that had pitched me into some earlier century.

Somewhere in the depths of the pine forest beyond the lawn, a dog barked, startling me. Of course there was no reason why the guard dogs should not be patrolling the grounds by day as well as by night, and probably every reason why they should. Especially when Mr Oversall was in residence.

A wrought-iron bench at the edge of the pine trees seemed a likely destination. I could sit there and look as though I were resting, while keeping the entire forecourt under observation.

Dr Anderson's car was still parked by the front door, telling me that he hadn't left yet. Although it wasn't his usual day for doing his rounds, he might be checking his patients just the same, since he was here anyway. But why was he so insistent that I keep out of the way?

The dog in the forest barked again – or was it a fox? Another dog howled in answer. What was the matter? Was there an intruder? I glanced over my shoulder, but could see nothing untoward.

A low growl at my feet made me snap my head around to find a large German shepherd sniffing at the hem of my kaftan.

I froze.

'Steady on, Brutus. It's only Miss Vanessa. You know her.' I was relieved to see the dog was attached by a businesslike chain to one of the guards.

'Oh, Brutus,' I said feebly. 'Hello, Brutus.' That was the trouble: he knew Vanessa – he didn't know me. And he didn't look as though he'd be as reasonable about it as Gloriana had been.

Another growl and Brutus raised his head, sniffing up to my knees and heading unerringly, in the way of the beasts, for my crotch. I realized just how much I had always preferred cats.

'Down, Brutus!' A sharp yank on his choke chain momentarily discouraged the monster. 'He doesn't mean anything by it,' the guard apologized, disregarding further growls. 'He just hasn't seen you for a bit and wants to check you out.'

That was what I was afraid of.

'We found you, you know, Brutus and me,' the guard went on. 'Brutus, really. Sniffing and yelping and pulling me down into the moat. There you were, all blood and mud and dead white. I wouldn't have given a tinker's damn for your chances, but you've scrubbed up real well. How are you feeling?'

'I've felt better.' I fended off another of Brutus's advances. He was practically in my lap. I wondered if he would snap my hand off if I pushed his muzzle away.

'Not surprising.' The guard nodded and pulled Brutus back again. 'They tell me you can't remember anything about it.'

'That's right, I'm afraid. But I can't thank you enough, Mr . . .'

'Bud, just Bud,' he said. 'No thanks necessary. Just doing

my job. And Mr Oversall gave us a nice bonus – best steak for Brutus and an extra month's wages for me. Glad we got to you in time.'

'So am I.' I shuddered. If Nessa had lain there much longer, her chances would have been nil.

Sudden activity over on the forecourt drew my attention. The front door had opened and Dr Anderson emerged in a far more leisurely manner than he had arrived.

'Why there's Dr Anderson,' I said in innocent surprise. 'But this isn't one of his usual visiting days, is it? What's going on, do you know?'

'Oh, usual hysterics and such. Houseful of women – what do you expect?' He shrugged uncomfortably. 'One of the silly little cows tried to top herself.'

'What? Who?'

But he had tugged at Brutus's chain and they were walking away at a brisk clip. Too brisk for a supposed invalid to catch up with them.

Chapter Nine

Before I was halfway across the sitting room, I knew I was in trouble.

Gloriana stalked forward, nose quivering, whiskers twitching, fur bristling. Her accusing glare brought on an attack of instant guilt – and I didn't even know what I had done.

I was going to find out. She advanced relentlessly, upper lip curled back, nose working overtime.

'What's the matter with you?' But I knew. *I* was the matter.

She stopped in front of me, just out of reach, and gave me *that* look. The look of a betrayed bride whose husband has just reeled home reeking of gin and another woman's perfume. And with lipstick on his collar.

'Now look –' I followed her gaze and saw the damning evidence of dog hairs sprinkled all over my kaftan.

That was it. I was guilty of consorting with the enemy. Treason, treachery and betrayal. The evidence was in clear sight, even for those with no sense of smell.

'It wasn't my fault,' I said. 'I can explain. I didn't encourage him. I don't even like him.'

That's your story! She turned away, her tail jerking upwards in the feline version of a two-fingered salute, and stalked away. The divorce papers were in the post.

I hurled the offending kaftan into the laundry bag and donned a fresh, uncontaminated one.

She'd come round. Wouldn't she?

* * *

There was a full complement at dinner that evening, I was relieved to see. Either someone had made a quick recovery, or the 'silly little cow' was a member of staff.

Even Madame was already at the table when I arrived, not inordinately late. In line with Monica's suggestion that I could use some extra rest, I had skipped the drinks session in the library.

There was a low murmur of greetings as I took my seat, then the silence descended again. It appeared that they all had a lot to think about.

So had I.

Two women had now nearly lost their lives in this establishment. Surely that was above the law of averages.

Was there a connection between them? Probably. It was too much of a coincidence, otherwise. Especially as there had been an abortive initial attempt to pass off Nessa's fall as an attempted suicide.

Not much imagination being used, then. And the attempt bungled both times.

I looked down the table at Ivor. Incompetence, thy name is Beloved.

Sensing that he was being watched, he raised his head abruptly and met my gaze with a sickly smile.

I looked away hastily. There might be things one had to do in the line of duty, but I wasn't sure I was ready for them yet.

'And how are you this evening, Madame?' I asked softly.

'I survive.' She shot me a bleak look. 'I advise you to do the same.' She pushed back her chair and rolled away. Richie immediately rose and followed her.

Her exit passed unremarked. Perhaps it was her usual manner of leaving. She seemed to have eaten most of her meal and no one bothered about desserts around here. If I could manage a trip into town, I was going to lay in a stock of chocolate bars. Man does not live by entrées alone.

Surprisingly, Ivor was the next to leave. Did that mean

he'd be waiting in ambush for me in the cloister? I decided to join the others for coffee tonight. Let him cool his heels literally in the chill wind that swept along the monks' walkway.

On the theory that the description 'silly little cow' could best be applied to one of them, I carried my coffee over to the corner where Kiki and Nina were sitting. Was it my imagination that hostile looks seemed to follow me?

'Mind if I join you?'

There was a flutter of surprise, then agreement. As usual, they were huddled at the back, near the false bookcase that provided their emergency exit. Nina threw an anxious glance towards it as I sat down.

They both looked much the same as when I had last seen them. No shadows under the eyes, no pallor or nervous twitches. In fact, they looked better than I did – but my appearance was largely due to heavy make-up. They were wearing the minimum.

'You're looking better,' Kiki said; the inspection had been mutual. 'Are you?'

'I think so.' I smiled wanly, then remembered that I was supposed to be improving enough to wangle a trip to town. 'I'm feeling a bit stronger . . . physically, anyway.'

'Oh, good!' Nina said. 'Then you must come to tea with me tomorrow and see my studio. You know, you promised you would.'

'Mmm . . .' I was sure I hadn't agreed to anything so definite, but it might not be a bad idea. I had to start moving around and learning more about the place.

'And you, too, of course.' She looked at Kiki, who seemed no more enthusiastic than I was, but obviously didn't want to miss anything.

'If you're sure it's no trouble . . .' I said.

'Oh, none at all,' Nina assured me. 'I'll just let Monica know and she'll send everything along.'

'Monica is so good about that.' Was there a trace of irony – mockery – in Kiki's voice? Her face was expressionless.

'Isn't she?' Nina agreed wholeheartedly. 'It's so wonderful here. All you have to do is ask for something – and it's yours! Almost like having a magic genie. This is the perfect place for an artist!'

'Isn't it?' Unmistakably, there was a wry twist to Kiki's mouth.

A soft riff of melody swirled across the room and I saw that Yvonne had seated herself at the grand piano in the far corner and was moodily picking out one of the songs that had earned her that brief fame. 'Songs of Yesteryear' they would be called now.

Another faint sound behind us brought Kiki to an upright alert position. She didn't turn, but it was obviously an effort not to. Nina cast a nervous glance over her shoulder, then another at me to see if I'd noticed anything.

Of course, I hadn't. I was watching Yvonne raptly, giving no indication that I had heard that faint click of a latch being released on the concealed door, or the other faint click as the door closed again.

They both relaxed. I hadn't noticed a thing. Not the heads rigidly refusing to turn, not the tensed muscles of legs that wanted to spring into action. I was as innocent – dumb – as they hoped I would be.

'She's so talented,' I purred, all my attention still on Yvonne, who had begun to subvocalize softly along with the music. 'Such a pity that she, um, retired so early.'

'Isn't it?' Kiki's lips quirked again. 'And she's such a sweet person, too.' The look she exchanged with Nina said that there was a lot they could tell me about Yvonne – if I asked the right questions. But not here, not now.

That was all right with me. There were plenty of other questions.

'I saw Dr Anderson arriving this morning. I thought his visiting days were Tuesdays and Fridays. He seemed to be in quite a hurry. Nothing wrong, I hope?'

'Not seriously,' Kiki drawled. 'One of the maids went off the deep end and needed a bit of seeing to. Nothing to do with any of us.'

Just one of the hired hands. So that was all right then. I wondered where Nessa stood in their scheme of things: one of the entourage or another of the hired hands?

'I'm glad it wasn't the one who cleans my studio.' Nina was completely self-absorbed. 'I've just got that one trained to leave things alone. They may look messy to her, but they're meant to be that way.'

'That's what you always say,' Kiki taunted. 'The state of your studio betrays a mind that –'

'I've got to get back to work now.' Nina stood abruptly.

'You always run away just when the subject threatens to become interesting.' Kiki tilted an eyebrow. 'And the excuse is always your work. Doesn't that suggest anything to you?'

'And what work do *you* do?' I cut in quickly. It was as near to a cue as I was obviously going to get.

'I'm working on a book. You don't even remember that?' Kiki was incredulous. 'When we've talked about it so much? When you've agreed how important it will be?'

I shrugged, revising my earlier opinion: they were *all* self-absorbed around here.

'Kiki –' Nina leaned over me, half-whispering, a glint of malice sparking in the depths of those dreamy eyes. 'Kiki is writing Mr Oversall's autobiography for him. She's a ghost!'

Another one? There were a lot of them around.

'How interesting.' I kept my face and voice bland.

'A ghost with a psychology degree,' Nina emphasized.

'Everett is very interested in psychology,' Kiki said. 'And it's not quite an autobiography, it will be more about his business philosophy, the structure of power, the climb to the top, the people along the way. He intends it to be inspirational to the younger generation coming along and . . .'

Mmm-hmm. There was a lot of that around, too. I tuned out on what was obviously a well-rehearsed justification of her position here.

It was interesting to know that Everett Oversall intended to join the ranks of business tycoons who were writing How-To-Be-As-Successful-As-I instruction manuals. I wondered how many secrets he was willing to give away. Apart from his brief early flirtation with the gossip columns, he had never been very forthcoming about himself or his interests. Perhaps Candy Shaeffer had talked him into it as a good public relations move.

'When is it coming out?' I asked, when Kiki appeared to have run down. At least, she had stopped talking.

'When I finish it.' Her lips tightened.

Nina snickered.

'Having problems?' I tried to sound sympathetic. 'How long have you been working on it?'

'After the first six months, she moved in here with us,' Nina said helpfully.

'Everett thought it would be more convenient for me to be close at hand,' Kiki said. 'He told me I'd also find the others of great help to me with background material and additional research. That wasn't quite . . . accurate.' I got the impression that she was grinding her teeth. 'There are still so many questions and, no matter how I phrase them, I can't get straight answers.'

'Mmm . . .' It occurred to me suddenly that not all the hostility I had felt directed at this corner of the room had been aimed at me. I rephrased a question myself: 'How long have you been here?'

'Two years – but I've been helping in other ways, as well. It's just that it's so difficult to pin anyone down, including Everett, he's always so busy. But I must have him speak to everyone again and tell them to cooperate with me.'

There was a small, quickly suppressed gurgling sound from Nina.

'I'm sorry I didn't get a chance to see Dr Anderson.' Time to change the subject. 'I would have liked to beg a ride into town with him.'

'Are you sure you're feeling well enough?' Nina's concern did not quite mask the quick look she exchanged with Kiki. 'If you want anything, just speak to Monica. She'll arrange it.' With a faint smile, she turned and was gone.

'You really *do* have amnesia –' Kiki gave me a cool contemptuous look – 'if you can't remember that you're living in the most luxurious Open Prison in the country.'

Chapter Ten

She was only a bird
In a gilded cage . . .

The old music hall melody was swirling through my mind
when I awoke in the morning. Perhaps I could find a way
to incorporate it into the act – in a Mae West-ish sort of
parody . . .?

With vassals and serfs
By her side . . .

I trilled experimentally.

The cat gave me a filthy look: she was neither a vassal
nor a serf. Furthermore – she moved to put some distance
between us – she was not by my side, nor did she intend
to be. Yesterday's perfidy was neither forgotten nor
forgiven.

Yesterday . . . No, that was another song. Another problem. What had happened yesterday . . . and to whom . . .
and why?

Damn Anderson! Why hadn't he told me anything? He
must know there was a high probability that the two
events were connected. How much was Overall paying
him for his 'loyalty'? His silence?

I threw myself together quickly, then spent so long waiting that, when Dilys brought my breakfast, it was clearly
intended to be brunch. Except that it wasn't Dilys – and
there went that cosy gossip I'd been planning. I'd never
seen this one before and she wasn't the friendly type.

'Good morning.' She swept past me, set the tray down on the table and was gone again before I could say anything. So much for my plans to find out more about any below-stairs dramas. Oh, well, at least I could eat.

I could eat. I lifted the cover to reveal a luscious mélange of fresh fruit – two kinds of melon, strawberries, kiwi fruit, peaches, blueberries, pineapple, grapes – and a selection of miniature croissants and vari-seeded rolls. It all looked delicious, so why was I feeling so uncomfortable?

I looked away from it and met the furious disappointed eyes. There wasn't a thing here a cat wanted to eat. I had just added insult to injury.

'Look, I'm sorry,' I said. 'It isn't my fault. I didn't choose the menu. This is just what they brought me today.'

A likely story! She was quivering with indignation. I had done it again.

'You can have the coffee cream,' I placated. 'All of it. I'll drink mine black.'

Her ears twitched. Not good enough.

'And I'll see what I can scrounge for you at tea.' Belatedly, I realized that I had no certainty at all that tea at Nina's wouldn't run heavily towards alfalfa sprouts, wheat germ, and strange oddments juiced out of all recognition. Although, I remembered thankfully, Monica would be supplying the tea, so perhaps it wouldn't be that bad. 'Anyway, I'll do the best I can.'

It was an empty promise and she knew it. She continued to glare at me until I went over to the store of cat treats and opened the most expensive tin of cat food on the shelf. I also shook an over-generous amount of her favourite crunchies into her bowl.

Even then, she wasn't letting me off the hook. She preferred people food – and I knew it. She was still staring moodily at her untouched goodies when I left for that tea with Nina.

Nina was in a better mood, which wasn't saying much. Ghengis Khan would have been in a better mood than that bloody cat. I could only be grateful she couldn't talk. If she could, she'd have shopped me for sure.

'There, now,' Nina beamed at me, 'isn't this nice? It's so good to have you here again. Just the way it used to be!'

'Is it?'

'You still don't remember?' Her brow rippled with concern. 'You can sit in that chair, just where you always used to sit, and nothing comes back to you?'

'Sorry . . .' I gave a hint of a shrug. 'They say it may never come back . . . and there's nothing I can do about it. Just wait . . . and see.'

'Oh, dear.' She bit her lower lip. 'I was *so* hoping . . .'

I let her dangle there while I looked around the room. It was slightly unnerving to find it so familiar. Had I unknowingly received some ESP transmission from Nessa – perhaps while in a dream state?

The parade of blue-and-white china across the mantel, the mirror above it, even the tall jardinière sparsely filled with peacock feathers by the side of the fireplace . . . I had seen them all before. It was as though I had walked into a Victorian painting.

And so I had, I realized abruptly. That was where I had seen it all before. So much for Nina's creative ability. Her studio was a mix-and-not-quite-match take-off of every Victorian fad that had lasted long enough to be immortalized on canvas.

'You like it, I can tell.' She glanced around complacently, unaware that she had been caught out. 'You always did. That's why you were going to have me do your quarters.'

'Mmm . . .'

'I could do it any time, now that you're back.' She was a little too eager. 'And it might help to take your mind off . . . things.'

'But I don't want to get my mind off anything,' I reminded her. 'I want to get my mind back – and all the things I had on it.'

'Oh!' She hadn't thought of that. Or had she? A faint glint of speculation flickered in the depths of her eyes. 'But you can ask me any questions you want. About anything you want to know.'

'The trouble with that is, I don't know what I want to know. I don't know what questions to ask.'

'Oh!' I watched her absorb this. 'Yes, of course. I hadn't thought of that. Of course you don't!' She sounded pleased about it.

'It might help if –' A light tap at the door interrupted me.

'There's tea!' Nina sprang towards the door as though she hadn't eaten for days. I remained seated, but turned to watch.

My hope was dashed again. It wasn't Dilys delivering the trolley, it was the sullen one who had brought my brunch. She didn't linger here, either; nor did Nina seem to expect that she would.

'That looks interesting,' I remarked as Nina wheeled the trolley over to the table.

'All sorts of fancy sandwiches,' Nina said appreciatively.

'I thought it might be. Antoine has to do his French cooking at dinner for Mr Overall, but he likes to experiment with sandwiches and petits fours for tea.'

'I haven't seen Mr Overall at dinner yet,' I said, then realized someone else was missing. 'And you've only set the table for two now. I thought Kiki was joining us.'

'Oh, no, she cancelled. She often does.' Nina shrugged. 'She said she wasn't feeling well. A headache, as usual. You can't depend on her, you know.'

'Really?' I wouldn't dream of doing so. I wondered if Kiki was having another search of my quarters while Nina kept me occupied here.

'I . . . I don't like to talk about it . . . and ordinarily, I wouldn't . . .' *Oh, no, not much.*

'But?' I encouraged.

'But you ought to know. Well, you do know – you *did* – but you don't any more. So . . . I mean . . .' She faltered to

79

a stop, frowning, having got so convoluted she wasn't sure what she was trying to say any more.

'So, perhaps you ought to tell me,' I prompted. 'If you really think I ought to know. You do, don't you?'

'Oh, yes!' She had no doubt about that and was relieved that I had seen it so clearly. 'You *need* to know! Otherwise, you might . . . she might . . .' She broke off again in confusion.

'I see.' Although I didn't. I was beginning to suspect that confusion was her natural state.

'Maybe you're beginning to remember,' she said hopefully. 'Then it wouldn't be so embarrassing.'

'Don't worry about that.' Incompetent liars are always embarrassing. I waited for what would come next.

She still hesitated and I could see the twisting of a devious brain behind her eyes.

'Why don't you start at the beginning?' I encouraged. 'When I first arrived. You *were* here then?'

'Of course!' She was indignant. 'We all were. You only came just about a year ago. After Francesca ran off, leaving poor Everett in the lurch, with all the important projects he had pending. It was really rotten of her! Not that we weren't happy to have you here,' she added hastily.

'Francesca?'

'She came here from one of his Italian companies. Toffee-nosed little cow!' The sudden explosion of spite was unnerving. Nina seemed to recognize it and gave me an unconvincing smile. 'But her English was as good as her Italian. She must have been very useful – in business matters, of course.'

'Of course.' I didn't believe that any more than she did. I wondered which one of Everett Oversall's harem had felt the most displaced by Francesca.

'Not that Everett seems to miss her very much.' There was a muted glee in her voice. 'He's mostly annoyed that she left without any notice. That's why he was so delighted to find you to take her place so quickly.'

'I see.' That implied I was doing a satisfactory job. I would have expected nothing less of Nessa.

'Have another sandwich.' Nina leaned forward, holding out the plate of tiny crustless triangles. 'They're not very big –'

A sudden horrendous clatter drowned out her words and obliterated all thought.

'What's that?' I shouted over the racket.

'The helicopter.' Nina's voice rang out as the noise faded into the distance. 'The landing pad is over behind the trees.'

'Oh.' I settled back in my chair. I should have known this place would have the means for instant access – and escape – for someone like Everett Oversall. Road transport would be too slow. And possibly too hazardous.

'It really frightened you for a minute, didn't it?' Nina's eyes gleamed speculatively. 'Perhaps you're beginning to remember. The last time you heard that was when the air ambulance took you away to hospital.'

'I don't think I was hearing much of anything then,' I said bitterly. The image of Nessa's motionless shattered form rose in my mind. She still wasn't hearing anything.

'Oh, well.' Nina helped herself to another sandwich, since I wasn't going to. 'That means we'll have dinner in our rooms tonight. Most of us. Everett likes to entertain his important guests in private.'

'What guests?'

'The ones who arrive by helicopter. Who knows who they are?' She shrugged. 'Oil sheikhs, industrial magnates, world leaders, or – perhaps –' she gave me a sly smile – 'just some pretty lady who's caught his fancy. In any case, we aren't wanted at the party. Most of us . . .'

'Most of us?' It was the second time she'd said that. I can recognize a cue – especially when I'm being beaten over the head with it.

'Madame sits in on the business dinners. Later, Yvonne does her cabaret act.' Her mouth twisted. 'Then maybe

81

Amanda and Candy are there for the sophisticated conversation stuff, depends on who the guests are. If they were Italian –' the way she said it brought the word *Mafia* to mind – 'he wanted Francesca there. I think he got her to translate what they were saying between themselves for him later. And you filled in, too, recently.

'But I don't think you'll be called on tonight.' Her assessing gaze raked over me, from my bandage-turban to the shadowed bruises on my face and the wrist support bandage on my right wrist, which gave me an excuse if my handwriting wasn't exactly the same as it had been before the accident. 'You're not looking very decorative at the moment.'

'I don't suppose I am,' I agreed. 'I'm not feeling very sociable right now, either.'

'Never mind, the food is great when we have it in our own rooms.' She obviously thought she was cheering me. 'Then we get simple stuff. Steak and chips or fish and chips for us, while the kitchen turns itself inside out on fancy stuff to impress the guests. They don't want to bother with us. I like it better that way. Except for the times when they lock us in.'

'Lock us in?'

'Oh, it doesn't happen all the time. Just when there are really important people – the kind who bring their own armed guard and all sorts of security men with them. Everett says it's for our own safety, just in case any of them get trigger-happy. We're better off out of their way.'

Everett might be right. Presumably he knew the sort of people he was dealing with. There were a lot of paranoid dictators about and they usually surrounded themselves with fellow paranoics. The shoot-first-and-ask-questions-afterwards brigade.

'As though any of us were assassins!' Nina snorted. 'I'll bet that's not the only reason Everett keeps us locked up. The way some of those men stare at us when they think we aren't looking gives me the shivers. I feel safer being locked in.'

So did I, but it raised an interesting thought. If there were a master switch to lock us in from the outside, then doors we had locked from the inside could be opened by the same means. Perhaps there was more than one reason for the manual inner bolt on Nessa's door.

The clatter in the distance had died away and stopped. The deep throb of a powerful motor replaced it, heading towards us.

'Here they come now,' Nina said.

'Are we allowed to look out the window?' I asked. 'Or will we be turned to stone?'

'Oh, they won't come this close.' She sounded regretful. 'They'll go to the private entrance to Everett's quarters. People come and go that way all the time without any of us seeing them.'

Why did that not surprise me? Everett Oversall had transformed the Victorian fake monastery into a modern fortress; already remote and secluded, it was now heavily guarded and impregnable. He could entertain whom he liked, when he liked, without fear of observation.

Presumably. There were, of course, persistent rumours that he was the object of constant surveillance by most of the intelligence services of the world. He had never actually been caught in anything illegal – yet – but they lived in hope, just waiting their chance to pounce.

The telephone jangled sharply, startling me.

'My, you *are* jumpy,' Nina observed as she crossed the room to answer it. 'That'll only be Monica to ask whether we want steak or fish.' She picked up the phone and nodded confirmation to me.

'I'll have the steak,' she said into the phone. 'Wait a minute, I'll ask her.' She raised her eyebrows at me. 'Steak or fish?'

I thought of my little Duchess watching hopefully as the food arrived and didn't hesitate. 'Fish, please.'

'Did we have to ask?' Nina laughed into the phone and I sensed the laughter was shared at the other end. 'She's eating for two!'

There was a different – spiteful? – note in the gust of laughter following that remark.

I snapped to attention. Was it only the cat she meant? Or was there a double-double meaning? I tested the thought carefully: Nessa, pregnant? Me, an uncle?

No, not Nessa, I decided, surprised at the faint sense of loss I felt. Anything like that would have shown up in the medical report. In any case, no foetus could have survived that devastating fall. A miscarriage would have been noted in the records.

Unless the information had been suppressed.

Because Everett Oversall had ordered it to be? Or because the baby was Anderson's and he was covering his tracks?

'You look worried.' Nina's concerned tone was belied by the malice sparkling in her eyes, betraying that she had deliberately provoked the train of thought I was following.

Little bitch!

'Not at all.' I smiled serenely. 'I was just wondering how much of the fish my little darling will leave for me. She can be a bit greedy at times –'

The knock at the door was loud and demanding. We both jumped.

'Oh, it's you.' Nina sounded disappointed as she opened the door. 'I suppose you're on escort duty.'

'That's right.' Bud stepped into the room and checked that I was still there. 'We're letting the dogs loose early tonight. I'm to see her back to her quarters.' He looked at the table and then at me. 'You can finish your tea first.'

'I've had enough.' Of everything. I rose to my feet and thanked Nina for her hospitality before going with him.

She sighed as she met my eyes and nodded glum confirmation. They weren't wasting any time and that meant one thing:

It was going to be another locked-in night.

Chapter Eleven

At least the cat was happy. Tummy distended by a massive inhalation of crisp-battered cod, she sprawled on the bed, providing her own background music of contented purring. Who needed any other music?

Although I didn't doubt Nina's information, I tried the door and found it locked, despite my having unlocked it from my side. I turned my key again, relocking it as much as was in my power, although I knew now that that feeble power was easily overridden. I shot the bolt firmly, just in case the guests left before morning and we were released while we were sleeping. I didn't want any unexpected visitors.

So, an early night. Or, at least, a night when I could be sure of no interruptions. A good night to settle down with the depilatory creams, waxes and other tools of the trade and catch up with the maintenance routine.

I was doing my nails when I became aware of distant sounds. At first, I thought the Duchess had developed an interesting vibrato, then realized that there was a definite undercurrent of melody, plus words that sounded fervent, but indistinct.

The Duchess had also raised her head and was glaring towards the cloister walk, her tail twitching with irritation. They had disturbed her beauty sleep.

But she had given me confirmation that it wasn't just me who was hearing things.

The music intensified, but not very much; it remained

faint and ghostly. Ghostly, now there was a thought. I wondered if the Monk was parading the cloister, waiting for someone to become curious enough to step outside and follow him.

Seized with sudden suspicion, I tiptoed over to the door and tried to open it. Nothing happened. I remained safely locked inside.

Interesting . . . someone had their wires crossed. Either they didn't know that the minions were kept out of the way at certain times . . . or else they were taking advantage of that fact to bring in a portable sound system, knowing that I could not get out to investigate the source of the music, hoping that it would make me curious enough to follow the beckoning monk the next time he appeared.

Of course, there was another possibility. But . . . no. I couldn't believe that it was a genuine haunting. It was too calculated, too targeted.

A guard dog barked in the distance and was answered by another. The chanting cut off abruptly. It wasn't the first time they had barked, and they seemed to be getting closer. The spectral monk was obviously folding up his choir and making a getaway before they got to him.

I hoped the equipment was heavy and cumbersome and gave him a hernia.

On the other hand, given the ratio of males to females around here, the culprit could equally well be a female. That long bulky monk's robe could hide anything; it was almost as good as a kaftan.

The only certainty was that it was someone who hadn't been locked in. I thought immediately of Madame and amended the certainty: and someone who was mobile enough to get around swiftly.

The telephone rang suddenly and the cat spoke back sharply. Was there no peace around this place? She glared at me. It was obviously my fault.

I shrugged a disclaimer at her as I picked up the phone, wondering if this was my summons to join Everett

Overall and his important visitors. I didn't think it could be. Nina was right: I wasn't presentable enough right now – and I was determined to stay that way. Perhaps a heavier hand with the eyeshadow bruises?

'Hello? . . . Hello?' The only response was the soft click as the other end of the line hung up.

I replaced my own receiver thoughtfully. What was that all about? Someone ringing the wrong extension and too discourteous, or too unsure of his English, to apologize. Or someone checking to make sure I was still locked up in my quarters?

The cat's wary eyes and tensed attitude told me that the dogs, although silent, were closer now, perhaps sniffing along the perimeter of the cloister. I turned out the lights and moved over to the window, opening the inner shutter just far enough to allow me a narrow streak of vision. There was nothing to be seen within that limited range and to open the shutter wider would be to betray my presence. I closed it again and switched the dimmest lamp back on.

The cat was still tensed. Light, or the absence of it, hadn't affected her attitude: she was still suspicious, mistrustful and ready to disappear if the worst developed. She turned towards the cloister walk, ears pricked.

I froze and listened, too. It seemed to me that I heard a faint ominous growl outside. Then I definitely heard a low gruff command. Brutus and Bud. I had moved away from the window just in time.

'Everything all right in there?' Bud's voice called softly enough not to disturb me if I were already sleeping. Why wouldn't it be all right? He had personally delivered me to the door and seen me inside. The automatic locks must have clicked into place as soon as the door closed behind me. The question was automatic, not expecting an answer. Of course, I must be all right and fast asleep for hours.

As the footsteps retreated, the cat let her head fall back

and returned to sleep. All clear now. I sat up for another half-hour before joining her.

In the morning, the door was unlocked when I tried it. I heard the rain beating against the windows in a steady downpour and it seemed to me that sometime in the dark hours of the morning I had vaguely heard the clatter of a departing helicopter. Since we had now been released from our temporary imprisonment, it would seem that the visiting dignitaries had gone with it.

The unfriendly maid brought breakfast and would not be drawn on anything other than how long the rain might continue. She was not an optimist, either.

'All day, maybe all week,' was her verdict. It was November, after all.

Gloriana came to investigate the tray and turned away in disgust. The chef, perhaps exhausted by last night's efforts, hadn't bothered much this morning. A bowl of muesli and a pot of coffee. Or was he telling me something? Perhaps that it was time I recuperated enough to totter over to the breakfast buffet set up in the morning room. If so, the message wasn't going to get through. I'd rather go hungry than face the others first thing in the morning.

The cat had a different opinion. It wasn't good enough, she let me know. All that disruption last night, and then the rain, and now – starvation! If she had anywhere else to go, she'd leave home.

'I didn't order this,' I told her. 'I can't help what they decide to send me.'

She turned her nose up and sniffed. Then, suddenly alert, sniffed again. She leapt up on the table and moved forward purposefully, zeroing in on the covered butter dish beside the croissant.

I lifted the lid and there, nestling next to the curls of unsalted butter, were three cocktail sausages. Leftovers from last night's festivities, obviously.

Good old thoughtful Monica. I could grow quite fond of her – if she weren't getting to be one of my prime suspects.

Monica Chandler, who kept a watchful eye on every detail of the housekeeping. Monica, who knew everyone's foibles and, possibly, secrets. Monica, who had hurriedly packed and swept away all of Francesca's possessions before Nessa had arrived to take her place.

A gust of wind hurled a waterfall against the windows. This was going to be a day to remain as sequestered in our cloister – locked in or out – as any medieval cleric.

And possibly a good day to take closer stock of my surroundings and discover just how meticulous Monica had been in packing up the belongings of the previous occupant. To look for traces of Francesca.

If Monica had been careless enough to leave any. If there was anything to find. Anything of any importance. Anything that might have been overlooked. Anything . . . at all.

I sat down at the table and poured some milk over my muesli without enthusiasm. I inspected the first spoonful warily. It might be safer for the future to express a sudden craving for boiled eggs – boring, but tamperproof, boiled eggs.

Gloriana had no such qualms. She had helped herself to the cocktail sausages and, once she understood that I had no intention of disputing her right to them, was regarding me with approval. We were friends again.

For whatever that was worth around this place. I already appeared to have more friends than I knew what to do with. I did know what not to do with them: trust them.

Had they been such firm friends with the alien Francesca, too? Did she get together with Nina and Kiki for long girlish gossipy sessions? Was Ivor also *her* Beloved?

Somehow I doubted it.

Just as I doubted that Nessa had ever been so close to any of them, either.·

I pushed away the muesli and stood up. The cat gave me a sympathetic look, but stretched a warning paw over her remaining sausage just in case I had changed my mind. She might not be able to finish it right now, but it would make a tasty snack later.

After an hour and a half, I had to admit it had been a stupid idea. Too much time had elapsed, I was chasing shadows.

Francesca had disappeared over a year ago. All her belongings had been packed up and stored away by the ever-efficient Monica. I wondered where.

Then Nessa had moved in and made the place her own. There were unlikely to be any traces of Francesca still around. And nothing to tell what had prompted her sudden departure.

Had she, as Nina fantasized, eloped in the sudden throes of a romantic frenzy? Perhaps carried away, literally, in one of the helicopters belonging to a passing billionaire?

Or, more sinisterly, had the locks not served their purpose one dark night and had she been kidnapped by one of the thugs in uniform surrounding some dictator, sheikh or despot?

Or . . . had she followed the Monk?

The day continued grey and wet. The cat curled up and went to sleep. Lucky cat.

I was too restless to settle. My thoughts churned round in circles, getting nowhere. Or else dashing off in directions I did not wish to go.

Except for the rain against the windows, the place was silent. It might have been deserted, all occupants spirited away, the fake ruins left to disintegrate into genuine ruins.

Surely it had never been this quiet before. Although I had not been paying any particular attention, it seemed to me that I had been vaguely aware of muted domestic noises during other days: the hum of a vacuum cleaner, footsteps hurrying from one destination to another, the occasional bark of a guard dog or cry of a peacock, the dull throb of a motor as one of the estate cars drove past. There had not been this deep unnerving silence, this lack of evidence of any other humans in the world.

At this point, I'd even have welcomed the sound of spectral chanting again.

I moved to the window that looked out on the cloister and pulled back the curtain. Rain dripped from the eaves and the greensward beyond the walkway was beginning to show signs of the puddles forming in its hollows.

Wet, bleak and depressing. Suddenly, I needed air, however rain-laden. I draped the familiar shawl around me and stepped out into the cloister, locking the door behind me. I didn't want anyone slipping into my quarters while my back was turned even briefly.

It was colder than I had anticipated. I drew the shawl tighter. A chill wind swept down the cloister carrying the rain with it. The cloister wasn't as sheltered as it looked. What was? Puddles had formed in and around the uneven flagstones. I had to remind myself that the stones had not been worn down by centuries of monastic processions, of silent monks scurrying to the chapel or taking the air on a day like this. The whole construction was an elaborate Victorian fake. An edifice of lies and illusion. Ghostly monks included.

I reached the door leading into the main house, pivoted and walked back, deciding that I wouldn't stay out too long. The cold was all-embracing, even the soles of my feet were feeling the chill from the icy paving stones. The air had gone from bracing to arctic, seeming to have dropped several degrees in the short time I had been out here. My mood wasn't improving, either, it was as bleak as the world around me.

Nessa . . . I called silently and experimentally and waited . . . listening . . . as though there might be some reply.

There wasn't, of course. There couldn't be. Not now . . . perhaps not –

No! I wouldn't let myself think that. Nessa was a survivor. So was I. We'd had to be.

The deep shudder that suddenly racked me took me by surprise. It was visceral, rather than owing anything to the plunging temperature. Depression and dark thoughts were crowding in on me.

Where the hell was that quack, Anderson? Why wasn't he here to tell me how Nessa was doing? He'd promised to keep me informed. Had she lost ground, and was he afraid to face me and admit it?

Perhaps he was trying to reach me now. Would I hear it out here if the phone rang?

Odds were, I would. But he couldn't take the risk of telephoning – there were too many chances that someone might be listening in. He'd have to report personally. Eventually . . .

I shuddered again and moved forward. I'd just walk to the end of the cloister and back to my own door. I'd got my fresh air and honour was satisfied. There was no need to turn a stroll into an endurance contest.

I quickened my pace. Down to the anchorite's cell and turn back – and that would be my exercise quota for the day. I'd never gone in for the hours in the gym and the jog till you drop routines.

There! I reached my goal: the end of the cloister. I turned quickly, glancing idly into the cell to nod hello to the wax figure perpetually at its prayers.

I was three steps farther on before I did the classic double-take and retraced my steps. I must have been seeing things. It couldn't –

It could. It was. There were two figures in that cell now.

I wrenched at the bars, trying to open the gate, to get inside. I might have known it was useless. The bars held, the figures beyond them remained motionless and unreachable.

For a moment, I cursed, fluently and vehemently. The wax monk knelt, unheeding.

The female, lying face down, the back of her head imploded, hair colour obliterated by blood and bone, one arm outstretched, hand reaching toward the hem of the monk's robe, was clearly beyond help.

Chapter Twelve

'Are you sure?' Monica asked. 'Are you really sure?'

'It's not the sort of thing one is likely to make a mistake about,' I said coldly.

'No, but –' In the abrupt silence, I could almost hear the wheels turning and the contingency plans clicking into place in her mind.

'Where are you now?' she asked. 'Right this minute.'

'In my quarters,' I said. 'I came straight back and rang to let you know.'

'Right!' she said. 'Stay there! Lock the door! We'll be along straight away!'

'We –?' But she had rung off.

After half an hour, it was quite clear that Monica's definition of 'straight away' and mine did not coincide.

I had telephoned her again at the quarter hour and at five-minute intervals thereafter, but there had been no answer. I had no doubt that she was extremely busy somewhere, doing something. But what?

Impatient, I had tried to disobey orders and go back to the anchorite's cell for another look. That was when I discovered that the override lock had been flipped into place and I was locked in. The Open Prison had closed again.

There was nothing to be seen from the window, although I was sure I could hear muted sounds of activity at the end of the cloister. On the other side, there had also

94

been the throb of powerful motors: one or two cars arriving – and departing.

When the knock finally came, I played it straight, opening the door without hesitation, as though I had never tried it earlier and found it locked.

Sure enough, it opened easily. Monica stood outside and, behind her, Dr Anderson. *Nessa?* For a heart-faltering instant, I froze, staring at him.

No. He caught my fear and, behind Monica's back, he shook his head reassuringly. That wasn't why he was here. Of course not. It was the body in the anchorite's cell. I began to breathe again.

'Nessa, are you all right?' Monica stepped into the room, face creased with concern. Anderson followed. 'Really all right?'

'I'm fine.' I gave a shaky laugh, in keeping with my parlous condition. 'Well, a bit shaken . . . naturally.'

'Naturally.' Monica nodded, sending a meaning glance towards Anderson, who suddenly looked uncomfortable.

'Who was she?' I wanted to know. 'I couldn't get close enough to see. What happened?'

'You shouldn't have been out in weather like this. It's too cold and you're still too frail. It isn't good for you.' Monica moved forward, oozing sympathy. 'Why don't you lie down for a while and have a little nap?'

'Is it someone I know – or knew?' I backed away before she reached me. 'Not that I'd remember.'

'No, you wouldn't,' she agreed and frowned with increasing concern. 'Have you been having headaches lately? Or dizziness, or anything like that?'

'No.' I looked at Anderson. Shouldn't questions like that be coming from him? Except that he already knew the answers.

He looked away, visibly distancing himself from the situation. He didn't want to get involved. Too bad he already was.

'If you won't lie down, at least sit down.' Monica gave me what was obviously meant to be a reassuring smile,

95

then frowned at Anderson. 'Shouldn't you check her pulse?'

'Um, right.' Humouring her, he reached for my wrist while blocking her view with his body lest she notice that my hand against his was on the large side. 'A little fast, but within the normal range,' he reported.

'Are you sure?' That wasn't what she wanted to hear. He was letting the side down.

'I'm all right!' I snatched my wrist away. 'Just a bit shaken, that's all. It's not every day one finds a dead body.'

The silence was deafening. Monica looked at Anderson. Anderson looked back. Neither wanted to be the first to speak. Anderson turned his head, distancing himself even more, and Monica had to admit that she had lost.

'Nessa, dear,' she began. 'That's just it. You didn't. There was no dead body in the cell. That was just the wax figure, the way it always has been.'

Why was I not surprised? In the length of time between my informing Monica and their appearing here, they could have embalmed it, buried it and arranged for the memorial service.

'I saw her,' I said flatly.

'You *thought* you saw something,' Monica corrected. Her tone of sympathetic understanding was sickening. 'It's been a dark gloomy day, the cell is even darker, and filled with shadows . . .' She shrugged.

'Shadows don't bleed.' It wasn't Monica I was trying to convince. I avoided looking directly at Anderson, even as I wondered how much convincing he needed. There had been the sounds of several cars arriving and departing. When had the good doctor arrived: before or after the body had been spirited away?

'I don't think you quite realize, dear, just how seriously ill you've been,' Monica said.

Again, I was not surprised. If I'd thought about it, I would have taken a bet that that was the way they'd play it.

'You had such a terrible, terrible accident,' Monica went on. 'And you've made a remarkable recovery – so far. But you're still recuperating and it's not unusual if you've had a little relapse. Perhaps you've been pushing yourself too far, too soon. It's only to be expected that you might have some post-traumatic . . . difficulties. We do understand that head wounds can have that effect.'

'I was not hallucinating.' Anderson would know that. Monica could be excused – almost – for what she was pretending to believe. I wondered if tidying away bodies was a normal part of her housekeeping duties.

'Of course not,' she soothed. 'Vision problems are common in cases like yours.' She smiled forgivingly. She was winning and she knew it.

'But . . .' I closed my eyes and swayed briefly. 'But . . . I was sure I saw . . . something . . .' I had to let her win. For now. A barely recovered Nessa would not be strong enough, perhaps not sure enough of herself, to fight her corner.

'It's all right, we understand,' she cooed. 'You're over-tired. You mustn't think of trying to join us for dinner tonight. Have an early night and catch up on your rest.'

'Oh, but I've been resting all day.' I didn't want to miss dinner. I needed to speak to Madame – and to find out if anyone was missing from the table. 'It won't be too much for me. Truly.'

'I'm sure you think so, but I don't believe it would be wise.' The voice chilled, the velvet glove slipped. Monica was not about to let me mingle with the others. In the mood I was in, believing what I believed I'd seen, possibly asking awkward questions, I was a loose cannon and she was not going to have me rolling around.

'It would be best,' she went on firmly, 'for you to retire now and sleep through until morning. Everything looks so much better and brighter at the start of a new day. All the phantoms of the night will have faded away.'

'It's still early and I'm not at all tired.' That might be the way she'd like to have it, but I wasn't going to go along with it. Phantoms be damned! 'I'm feeling quite well enough to come to dinner.'

'No, that wouldn't be wise. You must conserve your strength.' She sent another meaning glance to Anderson. 'I'm sure you're a lot more tired than you think. Brian will give you a little something to help you go to sleep right away.'

'No!' I should have known that was why she had waited for Anderson to arrive before she appeared at my door. 'No! I'm not having *that!*'

'It's all right, Nessa, I promise you.' Anderson had drawn something out of his black bag and was smiling at me in a way I didn't like. 'Trust me.'

'No!' I saw light glint off a hypodermic needle and prepared to go down fighting. If he tried to roll up my sleeve, I'd lay him out. I could always claim that it had been a lucky punch. 'Try to touch me and you'll regret it!'

'Nessa, don't be silly. You see –' Monica spoke across me to Anderson – 'she *is* hysterical.'

'I am *not!*' Although there was plenty to be hysterical about. The mere thought of being left here unconscious, unable to throw the bolt against invaders, at the mercy of anyone who might have a key, made my blood run cold. As did the fear that Monica might decide I would sleep more comfortably if she were to undress me and put me into one of my nightgowns . . .

'All right,' I capitulated. 'I'll go to bed now. I'll take a sleeping pill. I've got some. I don't need anything from –'

I felt the sharp stab of the needle. Anderson had rammed it through my clothes, straight into a buttock. I tried to pull away, but it was too late.

What had he shot into me? The effect was almost instantaneous. I felt my muscles weaken, my eyesight blur, as I fought to hold on to consciousness. It was a losing battle.

'It's all right . . . Nessa.' He caught me round the shoulders in a strong grip and Monica advanced to steady me on the other side as they took me into the bedroom.

'Don't worry,' Anderson crooned. 'Just relax . . . trust me.'

As though I had a choice.

Tr-r-ru-u-u-s-s-t m-e-e-e . . . T-t-r-r-u-u-s-s-t m-e-e-e . . .
The words eddied and looped through my uneasy dreams, sometimes loud and demanding, sometimes soft and insinuating.

I was stumbling through a swirling fog that obscured my surroundings and blotted out the path beneath my feet.

Trr-r-u-u-s-s-t m-e-e-e . . . A disembodied hand thrust through the mists, extended towards me.

I reached out tentatively, only to recoil as a burst of high-pitched mocking laughter rang out behind the veiling fog.

I turned, disorientated, then turned again to find myself facing a mirror. I grimaced at it, but it just gazed back sadly.

It wasn't a mirror, it was Nessa.

'I trusted,' she said, *'and look what happened to me.'*

'Nessa . . .' I struggled through quicksands towards her, but she dissolved into the mist, leaving me bereft.

'Nessa . . .' I called after her. But she wouldn't come back.

'Nessa . . .' She had to come back. She *had* to.

Half-conscious now, I fought against restraining bonds. Had they tied me up? I felt again the sting of a needle – no, multiple needles. No, not again! I pulled away, managed to sit up and opened my eyes.

In the dim glow of the night-light that had been left burning, I saw two furious eyes glaring back at me and a paw raised to strike again.

The sheet was tangled about me, but I was still in my kaftan. Perhaps I could trust Anderson – at least, as far as I could throw him. This time. I was conscious, becoming more so with every minute – and with no drug-induced hangover. Only the lingering depression from the haunting dream.

'Down, girl,' I said. The cat looked at me uncertainly. Taking a risk, I rubbed behind her ears. Gradually, she lowered her paw and relaxed. She was still in an aloof mood, however. She must have been curled up beside me on the bed when I began to thrash around and disturb her.

It had given her a nasty shock – and I had the marks to prove it. I looked ruefully at the scratch just above my wrist, then pulled down the kaftan sleeve to cover it. And we had been doing so well, too. Still, a little setback could happen to anyone. As Monica had reminded me.

The bedside clock told me I hadn't been unconscious all that long. There was still time to join the others for dinner. Since that appeared to be what Monica had been determined to prevent, I decided I would.

I wanted to see which of the harem was missing – and what explanation might be given for her absence.

Chapter Thirteen

I showered and changed into a fresh kaftan, then waited until I knew they would all be in the dining room. As I went down the corridor, a familiar figure appeared at the far end, obviously having delivered his usual message.

'Don't tell me, let me guess,' I said when the black-clad young man drew abreast. 'Mr Oversall will not be joining us tonight.'

'You ought to know.' His icy glance raked me contemptuously. With elaborate formality, he stepped to one side and bowed me past.

'And what do you mean by –?'

He was gone. Disappearing into the shadows of the long dark passageway. Only the faint emanations of his hostility quivered in his wake to disturb the atmosphere.

Nessa, Nessa, what did you do to him? Would I ever know? Even if – when, *when* – she recovered, she might not reveal it. Close as we were, there were still some things we didn't tell each other. Whether we guessed or not was another matter.

I paused outside the door. The temptation to burst in on them in a dramatic entrance, appearing suddenly in their midst like the Demon King – or Queen – was strong, but I resisted it.

Low key was best. As if nothing at all had happened. Just another quiet dinner on another quiet day. Everything normal and routine.

Quiet – that was it. It was far too quiet in there. Profoundly, sadly quiet.

Who were they in mourning for?

I took a deep breath and slipped into the room silently, looking around to find out.

Think again.

The table was set as usual, but half of the usual diners were missing. Wide spaces yawned between the few who were seated there.

Which *one* was missing? Hell! Half of the females were missing. Any one of them might be the victim I had stumbled over.

'Nessa!' Monica looked up as I slid into the chair beside her and was not pleased. 'I told you –' She broke off as the curious faces turned towards her and forced a smile. 'Are you feeling better?'

'Much.' I smiled back. 'When I woke from my nap, I was feeling so much stronger, I decided to join you after all.'

'We're so glad you did.' Beloved spoke up. 'As you can see, our ranks are considerably reduced. Everett had another sudden descent of VIPs and sent for reinforcements.'

Richie was sitting on my other side, in Madame's usual place. He looked up and nodded hello.

I nodded back. Not for a moment had I thought the body might be Madame's. It was younger – and straighter – than hers.

'He sent for Yvonne and Amanda and Candy.' Grievance throbbed in Nina's voice. 'Even Kiki!'

'Not Candy,' Monica corrected. 'She's come down with one of her migraines. We may not see her for a couple of days now.'

Oh, really? I carefully kept my face blank.

'Rather odd, don't you think, the way Candy develops these convenient migraine attacks whenever Everett has certain visi –'

'That's quite enough, Ivor!' Monica called him to order.

But he had made his point. There were certain times when Candy chose not to get involved. Obviously, this was one of them.

'And you really *did* sleep well?' Monica turned back to me, oozing sympathy and, incidentally, changing the subject. 'No more . . . bad dreams?'

More? The word was insidious, implying a constant, ongoing and deplorable condition. Right up there with: *Have you stopped beating your wife yet?*

'If there were, I don't remember them.' I played along with a sweet smile, adding for good measure, 'This whole day seems to have gone all fuzzy and dreamlike.'

'You don't understand how ill you've been – and this gloomy weather doesn't help.' It had been the right thing to say, suggesting disorientating side-effects from that injection. Monica gave a small approving nod. Whatever Anderson had given me had done a good job.

'Winter gets so dreary here,' Nina complained. 'Now that it's set in, all the days seem to blend into each other. There are times when you don't know whether you're really awake or sleepwalking.' That earned her a nod of approval, too.

A young girl I hadn't seen before appeared and set a bowl of fragrant leek-and-potato soup in front of me.

And that brought another question to mind: how many servants *were* there around this place? Silent, swift and beautifully trained, they moved around so unobtrusively it was too easy to overlook them.

Was it one of them I had seen sprawled in the anchorite's cell?

'Eat your nice Welsh soup,' Ivor said. 'There's lamb hotpot to follow. Chef has gone back to his ethnic roots tonight.'

'Just the job for a night like this,' Richie observed. A gust of wind slammed against the building and a chill draught eddied through the dining room, underlining the truth of this.

The soup was delicious and the prospect of lamb hotpot sounded even better. Let Ivor sneer. Richie was right. Weather like this was just what Welsh country cooking had been created to combat and protect against.

The empty soup bowls were whisked away and replaced by the lamb dish. Only the clink of cutlery against china broke the silence. I glanced around at the others.

Monica was frowning at her plate. Richie was shovelling in the lamb, enjoying it and unconcerned about anything else. Both Nina and Ivor were pouting, although that wasn't slowing down Ivor's intake. Nina was pushing her food around the plate as though wishing it was something else, perhaps the more exotic sort of meal she imagined our missing colleagues were enjoying with the boss and his important visitors.

But were they really? If Everett Oversall had visitors tonight, they were evidently on the lower side of the danger scale. The rest of us were not being subjected to a lock-in.

Did that mean that it was unimportant if we happened to see and recognize any of them? Or did it mean that 'visitors' was an excuse – a code – to cover for something else?

Like a domestic Council of War?

That would explain why Nina and Ivor weren't wanted. I wouldn't trust them with any sensitive information, either. And I didn't blame Candy for not wanting to be involved.

They were probably trying to decide what to do about me. Not to mention the body I had discovered.

'Are you sure you're quite all right, Nessa? You look – *oh!*' Monica broke off with a little gasp, staring at me wide-eyed, one hand flying to her throat in response to the primeval instinct to protect the jugular vein when threatened.

Ooops! I realized I had inadvertently skewered her with the look I normally reserve for drunken hecklers. That would teach her to disturb my concentration! But she had no idea what she had done.

'I . . . I don't know . . .' Quickly, I fell back into character – Nessa's character – widening my own eyes. 'I just felt so odd . . . for a moment there . . .' I patted my forehead with my napkin. 'I'm sorry. I'm afraid I . . .'

'You're trying to do too much, too soon.' Monica was back in control, accepting my explanation, welcoming it. The more weakness I betrayed, the more anything I might have seen or thought could be discounted.

I smiled apologetically and managed three more mouthfuls of the succulent lamb before she spoke again.

'We'll excuse you from coffee, the last thing you want right now is any caffeine, a good night's sleep is more like it.' *And the sooner, the better*, her tone implied. 'You'll feel better in the morning.'

'Yes, probably,' I agreed. There wasn't much left on my plate and I'd learned not to expect dessert. I pushed back my chair, I might as well leave.

'I'll see you to your room,' Beloved said eagerly, too eagerly.

'Don't bother.' To my relief, Richie also pushed back his chair. 'I'll see to that.'

'Yes, thank you,' I said gratefully.

He winked and some of my gratefulness evaporated.

'Just a minute –' Monica caught up a saucer and scraped the remaining gravy and bits of lamb from my plate, adding a generous chunk from her own plate. 'You don't even remember how fond Gloriana is of lamb,' she said, handing it to me with a forgiving smile.

'Oh, dear! I'm afraid I don't.' I took it from her, grateful again. I had forgotten all about the bloody cat. I was going to have to watch that.

Richie stepped back, allowing me to precede him. A swift backward glance revealed Nina watching us jealously and Ivor pouting again. Monica had returned to staring at her plate with an abstracted expression, obviously thinking of more important matters. Undoubtedly, I figured largely in them.

Richie remained a step or two behind me all the way to the cloister, although I'd slowed my steps to let him catch up. Was this to underline the fact that he was more of a hired hand than I was? Or was he guarding my back?

Perhaps he was just shy. No, the wink he had given me blew that theory out of the water. It had been almost conspiratorial. What did we have to conspire about?

I wasn't going to find out that night.

'I'll wait here –' he stepped back at my door – 'while you take a quick look around to make sure everything's all right, then I'll go back and report that you're home safe.'

'Thank you.' How interesting to learn that Richie seemed to be aware that there might be a reason to make sure my quarters were safe before he abandoned me to them. What did he know that I didn't know – or suspect? And how could I pry it out of him?

'Hurry up.' He stepped gingerly over the threshold, leaving the door open behind him.

I started forward cautiously when a sudden streak of white lightning flashed past my ankles. Gloriana – sighting the open door and heading impulsively for freedom.

Freedom – with Bud and Brutus and all the other guard dogs out there patrolling the grounds.

'Don't let her out!' I made a dive to intercept her and missed. 'Shut that bloody door!'

'Well, well, well.' He blocked her way with his foot and scooped her up. 'Feeling a bit stronger, are we?'

'Galvanized by terror!' I snapped. 'If she got out – if those dogs got hold of her –' I didn't have to fake it, I felt genuinely faint and queasy at the thought.

'Sit down.' He was still holding Gloriana, who seemed to have given up all idea of leaving and was investigating his T-shirt with interest. I wondered if he had spilled any dinner on it.

'The door –' I said.

'If you insist.' He swung it shut with his foot, continuing to stroke and soothe Gloriana. 'I thought she was an indoor cat.'

'So did I. Unless that's something else I can't remember.'

'Females,' he shrugged. 'You're all fickle opportunists. You don't need to want anything. You just want to prove to yourselves that you can get it – whether you want it or not.'

Was he speaking generally, or had this conversation just taken a sudden personal turn?

'Typical male chauvinist,' I sniffed. That seemed a safe enough comment. 'I'm surprised Madame hasn't trained you better.'

'Are you?' His face closed down, he even stopped smiling at the cat. Certainly there were going to be no more smiles for me. 'Then I'd better get back to her, hadn't I, so that she can have another go at me.' He let the cat drop to the floor abruptly, where she looked as shaken as I felt at his sudden change of mood.

'Wait! I'm sorry. Don't go. I wanted to ask you if Madame –'

'Madame speaks for herself!' He was on the other side of the door now and seemed more comfortable there. 'If you don't remember *that*, then you'd better relearn it. And the quicker, the better!'

The door slammed shut behind him. I stared at it in bemusement.

'Who'd have thought the young man had so much fire in him?' I misquoted to the cat.

Who cared? She didn't. She had caught the scent of lamb from the saucer I still held. She rose up on her hind legs and spoke sharply.

'All right, all right.' I set it down in front of her. 'I'm sorry. I forgot all about it.'

She gave me one supercilious glance, then dived into the saucer with a dismissive flick of her tail.

Richie was obviously not the only one around here who thought I could do with a refresher course in the way I ought to behave.

Chapter Fourteen

I slept through most of the morning – or what passed for it in this gloom – and had barely finished my brunch when Nina arrived. Unannounced, uninvited and bearing a large portfolio which she dumped on the sofa table, beaming at me as she unzipped it.

'What's that?' I eyed it suspiciously.

'Sketches, swatches, proposals, plans.' She was proud of herself and whatever devilry she had packed into the large leather case.

'Nina, I'm sorry. I'm not really up to this yet.'

'All you have to do is look.' She swept any objections aside. 'You needn't make any decisions right away. This is just to give you something to think about.'

Just what I needed. Something to think about. At least she was assuming I could still think. I wasn't so sure some of the others would give me the benefit of that doubt, although they were ready enough to tell me what I should be thinking – and what I shouldn't.

'You'll love it, I know. After all, we *had* agreed –' She broke off and squinted at me assessingly. 'You still don't remember even one teensy-weensy thing?'

'Sorry.' I shook my head. 'Believe me, I wish I could.'

'Oh, I believe you. But it must be so awkward for you . . . and . . .' She hesitated delicately. 'And for the rest of us, too.'

'It's very difficult,' I sighed. She was angling towards something. I wondered if Beloved had enlisted her in his cause. Was I about to be supplied with spurious memories of the Great Romance? I might as well give her the opening she wanted; she was going to tell me anyway. 'I'm afraid there are all sorts of things I ought to be seeing to that I don't know about. Things that I ought to be doing . . .?'

'Well . . .' She waited for further urging.

'Is there something in particular you know about?'

'Well, actually . . .'

'Yes?'

'I wouldn't mention it, but I'd hoped you might remember before this . . . you promised so faithfully.'

'Promised what?' It was too fast, too sharp. She shrank back.

'I need to know.' I softened my voice and put a pleading look on my face. 'You must understand – it's so awful not knowing . . . especially if there were promises. I don't want to let anyone down – even though I can't help it, the way I am now.'

'Oh, I do understand!' She relaxed and forgave me. 'It . . . it's nothing, really. Well . . . not very much . . .'

'Yes? Tell me . . . please.'

She hesitated so long I wondered if I should try *pretty please*, but decided that would be going too far. I'd just outwait her.

'Well . . .' It wasn't such a long wait after all; she was dying to tell me. 'Actually . . . I don't want to rush you, or anything, but you *did* borrow some money from me and you were going to pay it back in a few days. Oh, I'm not blaming you. No one could have imagined what was going to happen, but . . . I *do* need to get more art supplies . . . and . . . and it was all my spare cash.'

'How much?' I kept my voice steady, my face concerned. Did I believe her or not?

'Well, t –' she flinched – 'three hundred pounds.'

'Three hundred pounds.' Why did I have the feeling that she had started to say 'two' and then upped the ante? Was she telling the truth at all? If Nessa had needed money, why hadn't she asked me?

'I'm so sorry.' I slipped into apologetic mode quickly. 'I had no idea.'

'Of course you didn't.' She forgave me, perhaps with a touch of relief that I hadn't questioned it. 'How could you, the way you were . . . are?'

'Yes, yes,' I said rashly. 'I'll see to it. Right away.'

But how? This was a complication I hadn't bargained on. Impersonating Nessa was one thing, forging her signature to dip into her bank account was something quite different. And if I took the money from the emergency funds I had hidden in my make-up box, it would leave me dangerously low.

'Only –' I looked at Nina's anxious face. 'I'm afraid I don't remember my bank – I know! I'll ask Monica.'

'Oh, no!' she said quickly. 'No! Don't tell Monica! This was just between us. We don't want her to know!'

That was the first statement from her that I believed.

Of course, if she was telling the truth, there wouldn't be enough money in Nessa's account, anyway. But I didn't believe Nina for a moment. She was trying it on – and I had to act unsuspecting and let her get away with it.

'I mean,' she went on swiftly, 'we're supposed to be able to manage on our salaries – small as they are. Everett gets very uptight about that. He even thinks we should be able to save, since he takes care of all our living expenses. Now, I don't know what you wanted the money for –'

'Neither do I.'

'And I didn't ask,' she continued firmly. 'I was glad to help, especially as you told me it wouldn't be for long. Neither of us could have foreseen what was going to happen to you. For all I know, you never even had time to spend the money. It might still be hidden away here somewhere.'

'I haven't seen any.' Was that why she and her chum had been prowling around in here when they thought the place was empty? Not looking for any money she had loaned Nessa, but because she thought Nessa had a secret hoard and she wanted to get her sticky little fingers on it.

110

Since that hadn't worked, she was now going to try to con it out of me. She had so much nerve that it was almost awe-inspiring.

'Speaking of salaries –' abstracted, I lapsed into theatrical slang – 'when does the ghost walk?'

'You –' Her eyes widened, her face lost all colour and she dropped the swatch of pale blue silk she had been toying with. 'You *do* remember!'

'No, I don't.' Her reaction startled me. 'Remember what? I remember nothing.'

'Then you've seen it! Since you've been back!'

'Seen what?'

'The ghost – you just said so! You wanted to know when you'd see it again. As though I could tell you!'

'What ghost?' That was not something I was going to admit. 'What are you talking about?'

'You asked when it would walk!' Her voice shook, she looked at me accusingly. 'You know!'

'Know what?' I widened my own eyes. 'I just used a bit of theatrical slang. It translates to: when do we get paid? It doesn't mean anything more than that. Not to me. What does it mean to you?'

'Nothing,' she said defensively. 'Not really. That is . . . you're sure you haven't seen it? Some of the maids claim they have – just before they give notice and leave.'

'Are you telling me this place is haunted? Not that I'd be surprised if there were a ghost or two here. It's that sort of place, isn't it?'

'You see? You feel it, too,' she whispered, as though there was someone nearby to overhear us. 'You *do* know. Even though you don't know you know. It's all coming back to you subconsciously.'

'No, it's not!' I had to knock this on the head before she started spreading it around and ruining everything. I repressed the thought that I'd also like to knock her on the head. Violence has never appealed to me, but I was beginning to think that, in her case, I could make an exception.

111

'You aren't looking at all well –' Abruptly, Nina began packing everything back into her portfolio. 'I've tired you. I'm sorry. I'm sure you ought to be taking a little nap now. I don't want to wear you out.'

'Perhaps you're right.' I slumped my shoulders and allowed myself to droop wearily. I might not have found out everything I could from Nina, but I had had just about enough of her company. 'I *do* feel exhausted. And I haven't been sleeping well,' I added for good measure.

'I knew it!' She was triumphant. 'You look awful, to tell the truth. Shall I have Monica send you dinner in your room tonight? She'll understand. She keeps telling us how fragile you are and that no one should bother you.'

Thank you, Monica. What a shame no one is paying much attention to your thoughtful instructions.

'Well . . .' Anything to get rid of her. 'I must admit I'm feeling more tired by the minute.'

'I could tell! Monica keeps reminding us that head injuries like yours are very dangerous things. She says they can have delayed repercussions and – just when you think you're all right again – they can come back on you and you have hallucinations and see and hear things that aren't there at all!' Her eyes gleamed greedily as she watched for my reaction. '*Have* you been having that trouble?'

'Have I?' I smiled back at her with an innocence that matched her own. 'If I have, I can't remember.'

'Oh, but I thought you'd only forgotten things that happened before you fell. Not things that have happened since you've been back.' She peered at me uncertainly. 'I mean, you still remember us now that you've met us all again – don't you?'

'It depends on what you mean by remembering. I know that I've just met you and the others in the last few days. Beyond – or before – that, I don't remember anything about you. Any of you.'

'Oh! And you're sure you haven't had any hallucinations? Seen ghosts . . . or strange things?'

'Not that I remember.' I smiled blandly.

112

'You're sure?' She seemed disappointed.

'How can a person without a memory be sure of anything?' I leaned back in my chair and closed my eyes. If she couldn't take that hint, I'd have to seriously consider throwing her out.

'Um . . . yes . . . I see . . .' There was a long dithering silence, which I did not break. 'Um . . . well . . .' I heard the door open and shut.

After a safe interval, I opened my eyes to make sure she was gone. She was. I got up and locked and bolted the door, then returned to my chair to think.

So Monica was planting the idea that I might now be subject to hallucinations, was she? And I'd thought she was a friend.

But Dear Monica ran the household and it was part of her job to get along with everyone – and it made things so much easier if everyone could consider her their friend.

However, Monica was a long-term paid employee of Everett Oversall. That was where her loyalty, possibly her genuine friendship – and who knew what else? – essentially lay . . .

'*Ooomph!*' I grunted as a furry object, unexpectedly heavy for its size, landed in my lap. I looked down and those bright sapphire eyes looked back at me expectantly.

'And where have you been lurking all afternoon?' I rubbed behind one fuzzy ear and she allowed it. 'Don't you like the company we keep?'

She blinked and turned her head away to stare pointedly at the jar holding her kitty treats.

'All right,' I agreed. 'I suppose you deserve it for being dispossessed all afternoon.' I got up and poured a lavish helping of munchies into her bowl, still musing my way towards an interesting conclusion.

Very interesting . . . and disturbing.

It seemed that, having failed to kill Nessa, someone was now trying to destroy the precarious mental balance she appeared to have achieved.

At best, they hoped it would undermine her credibility if she regained her memory.

At worst, they were preparing the way for another murder attempt, aiming for a verdict of 'Suicide, while the balance of her mind was disturbed'.

And the question was: did Monica really believe the story she was putting out? Was Monica a willing co-conspirator in the scheme or was she just – saving your presence, Duchess – just a cat's-paw?

Chapter Fifteen

I awoke next morning to the sound of seagulls crying and prison bars of light and shadow striped across the ceiling by the wan sunlight.

I lay there disorientated, taking a long moment to recall where I was – and why. Gradually, it returned to me: I was not in some seaside town with an evening performance to prepare for. I was in the middle of an ongoing private performance, my audience more sinister, and perhaps deadly, than a First Night filled with merely bitchy theatrical colleagues.

The seagulls – no, the peacocks – screamed again, as though in pain. Was Nina back on the prowl, forcibly collecting tail feathers? She'd better not let Madame catch her.

Madame. I had to speak to her today. She might not hold the key to the whole situation, but I felt certain she knew a lot of things it would help me to know.

And Dr Anderson was due for his rounds today. I had to corner him and get the latest report on Nessa's condition.

Nessa! I threw back the duvet and was startled by a muffled feline curse from its depths.

'Oops! Sorry, Duchess, I didn't know you were there.'

A pink nose poked out from a rumpled fold and there was a minor upheaval as the rest of her struggled free. She bared her teeth and spat out something I didn't want to translate, but which seemed to be along the lines of, 'Just watch it!' She glared at me and shook her rumpled fur

115

back into place before leaping to the floor and stalking off. In the direction of the food, I noticed.

Outside, the outraged cries sounded again, followed by the volley of barks that seemed faintly familiar. Brutus, I presumed.

Or possibly one of the other dogs. How many were there? I must ask Bud, he seemed to be the most approachable of the guards and wouldn't be surprised by my interest.

Human voices were raised in what was becoming a commotion. It was getting too loud for me to be able to pretend I had slept through. Besides, I was curious.

Kaftan and turban in place – and ignoring the indignant glare of the Duchess when she realized I was bypassing the food – I stepped outside, closing the door carefully and firmly behind me. She wasn't sneaking out, especially with dogs around.

The action was taking place on the other side of the cloister and I followed the sounds of an increasing discord. As I rounded the corner, I found them.

Sure enough, Nina had been at it again. Angry birds hissed at her, Brutus snarled in sympathy and Bud shook his head reproachfully.

'You shouldn't do it, Miss Nina,' he said. 'You know it will drive the old girl wild.'

'They were shedding them anyway,' Nina defended as best she could with her hands full of the evidence against her. 'Those feathers were trailing along the ground, almost out of their sheaths. It only took the tiniest twitch to get them, they just slid into my hand. It couldn't possibly have hurt Percy and Petruchio is an old crybaby anyway.'

'That's as may be, but I'll have to report it, you know. I have my orders.' He held out his hand.

'No!' Nina put the feathers behind her back. 'No, you can't take them. I need them.'

'Now, you know better than that.' He wriggled his fingers coaxingly. 'You've been told you can't keep them when you do that. You don't want me to fight you for them.'

Brutus growled in reinforcement.

'It isn't fair!' Nina cried. She looked around wildly and spotted me. 'Nessa, don't let him do it!'

What did she think I could do about it? I gave her my blankest look.

'Leave Miss Nessa out of this,' Bud ordered. 'She has enough problems without taking on any of yours.'

I nodded agreement, wondering just how much he knew about my problems – apart from the obvious.

For that matter, why was Nina lurking around the cloister? It was a fair distance from her studio. Was she really stalking the peacocks, or had she been delegated to keep an eye on me? Was she supposed to ingratiate herself with me and become my buddy?

If so, someone had made a serious mistake. So far as I was concerned, a little of Nina and her pretensions went a long way – and I'd already had more than enough.

Brutus decided to greet me by moving forward and thrusting his nose into my crotch. I backed away hastily.

'Stop that!' Bud commanded. 'That's no way to treat a lady. Bad dog!'

Brutus paid no attention, following me as I retreated, intent on pursuing his investigation.

'Horrid creature!' Nina sniffed. 'I don't know why we have to have so many of them around.'

'Security!' Bud snapped. 'If we didn't have them, you'd soon regret it.'

Brutus turned towards Nina and growled, sensing the criticism in the atmosphere. Bud bent to soothe him. Brutus lunged forward again.

'No, you don't!' It was not Brutus that Bud grabbed, but Nina, who was trying to sneak away with her feathers while he was distracted by the dog.

There was a brief scuffle, punctuated by shrieks from Nina and snarls from Brutus. Bud emerged as the winner, holding four peacock feathers, two of which had been

117

snapped in half and were drooping towards the ground. Their original owners had prudently disappeared by this time.

'Now you've done it!' Nina cried. 'Look at them – they're ruined! And I *needed* them! I hate you! I'd like to *kill* you!' She ran off.

'Nothing new there, then.' Bud winked at me.

'I'm afraid you've upset her.' I kept my tone and expression neutral, with an uneasy feeling that there had been something a little too intimate about that wink. And not to be encouraged.

'Nothing new about that, either. One or another of them is always upset around here.'

'It's colder than I thought.' I demonstrated with a shiver. 'I'd better get back inside. I just heard all the rumpus and wanted to know what was going on.'

'That's right, you need to keep warm.' He whistled to Brutus, who was advancing on me again with prurient curiosity. 'You have to take care of yourself.'

'Yes, I do.' In full retreat, I returned to my quarters, where the Duchess greeted me with deepest suspicion.

Damn Brutus! He must have left his scent on me again. And probably more than a few hairs. I brushed at my kaftan and tried to placate the cat.

'Brunch is coming right up.'

She sniffed and turned away. We were back to square one.

By late afternoon, I began to suspect that Anderson was not going to appear. At least, not to me.

Had any of his other unofficial patients seen him? Or was it just me he was avoiding? And why?

Because there was no news? Or because the news was so bad he daren't face me? I fought back the creeping anxiety, telling myself that I would know instinctively if anything had happened to my twin. Surely, I would know . . .

118

Meanwhile, his absence gave me the excuse I needed to drop in on Madame unexpectedly.

'I wouldn't bother her,' I explained to Richie, who was guarding the door, 'but I wondered if Dr Anderson might be here. I know it's one of his visiting days and he promised to bring me something for these headaches . . . head pains . . . I still get.' I gave him a brave uncomplaining smile.

'Mm, yes, I suppose you do.' He looked at my shrouding turban. 'How long until you get rid of the bandages?'

'He hasn't said. I'm hoping it will be soon. That's another reason I want to see him, to ask about it.'

'I'm afraid you're out of luck. No one has seen him. He hasn't been here today.'

'Oh.' I was suitably crestfallen. 'But I'd still like to see Madame.'

'Why?'

'Why?' I hadn't expected an interrogation. 'Why, just to see how she is, to talk, to have a little visit.' I stood my ground. 'I had the impression we were friends.'

'Oh, you did, did you?' His mouth twisted oddly. 'Don't pin any hopes on that. Madame is too old and too weary to have any friends. She doesn't trust people enough – and she's probably right. With Madame, armed neutrality is as good as it gets.'

'It seems to me,' I spoke more sharply than I had intended, 'that could be said of just about everybody in this place!'

'Too true.' He nodded. 'You're learning . . . or are you beginning to remember?'

When you remember, I'll be waiting . . . Had that message been from Richie? And, if he believed I was remembering, what was his reaction going to be?

'Richie . . .' Madame's voice called out behind him. 'Who are you talking to? Who is there?'

'That's torn it,' he said. 'She's awake now and she won't rest easy if she thinks she's missing something. You might as well come in.'

I followed him into the darkened parlour, blinking as he opened the curtains to let in what daylight there was.

'So, Vanessa, it's you.' Madame was propped up on a chaise longue near the fire. 'I might have known.'

'She insisted on seeing you, Madame,' Richie said. They exchanged a long look.

'Yes, she would.' Madame sighed faintly. 'Sit down, Vanessa. Richie, perhaps you would be kind enough to bring us tea.'

'No, really,' I protested quickly. 'I don't want to be any bother. I just wanted . . . to see how you were.'

'She was looking for Anderson,' Richie corrected. 'She thought he might be here.'

'And so he might. But not today.' Madame looked at me shrewdly. 'You are disappointed?'

'A bit. I'd thought –'

'He was supposed to be bringing her something for her head,' Richie explained, as though I couldn't speak for myself. 'She still gets aches and pains.'

'The tea!' Madame ordered sharply.

'Oh . . . right.' He nodded and left the room.

'That is better,' Madame said softly, as his footsteps retreated down the hallway and out of hearing. 'We have no need of an interpreter, you and I.'

'Haven't we?' I met her gaze innocently, feeling that the armed neutrality was all on my side. Was that the effect Richie had intended? Had he been putting me on my guard – or trying to destabilize any memories that might be surfacing?

'No!' Madame said firmly. 'Now perhaps you would care to tell me yourself: how bad is the pain?'

'Bearable,' I decided to admit. 'It comes and goes. But if there's anything he can give me to keep it away, I'd like to have it.'

'Naturally. That is what we would all like. To be as free of pain as possible. In the circumstances.'

'The circumstances . . .' I echoed. We looked at each

other. Her eyes were so shrewd I was glad that the little cottage parlour was so dark.

'Oh, Vanessa . . .' Madame shook her head and sighed deeply. 'Vanessa, Vanessa . . .'

'Oh, Madame . . .' I regarded her with equally resigned dismay and a great deal more frustration. Somewhere inside that twisted frame, behind those hooded eyes, was any amount of information I needed. I took a deep breath of my own and reminded myself that I couldn't shake it out of her, much as I might like to.

'Oh, Vanessa . . .' Her voice was mocking, but she gave me a long sad look. 'I did not think you were so greedy.'

'What?' Startled and shaken to the core, I was left breathless for a moment. 'What do you –?'

'Here we are!' Richie was back, a plate of miniature pastries in one hand, sugar bowl and milk jug in the other. 'Kettle will be boiling in a minute.' He took far too much time pulling over a small table and arranging the things on it.

'You should have brought a tray,' Madame criticized.

'Right! Sorry! Next trip.' He started for the door. 'Be right back.'

That was what I was afraid of. He didn't intend to leave me alone with Madame long enough to have any sort of conversation. Unless I worked fast.

'Madame –'

'You're right, this is easier.' He was faster. With a rattle of crockery and a clash of cutlery, Richie swept back into the parlour, dealing out cups, saucers, cake plates, tea-spoons and pastry forks.

He had brought three of everything, a clear declaration that he was going to join us, to monitor our meeting.

Obviously I was going to get nothing more out of this visit than a cup of tea and a badly thawed strawberry tart.

For a brief second, Madame met my eyes and I could not mistake the flash of annoyance – and warning. It threw a new light on to the situation. Perhaps it was not just me he distrusted, perhaps it was Madame.

Was he her nurse, her carer – or her jailer?

Chapter Sixteen

I had to appear unconcerned. Vague and unconcerned, that was the ticket. As though her decision didn't really matter greatly. But not too unconcerned.

'Monica, I'm beginning to feel terribly guilty,' I confided shyly as I accepted my preprandial glass of sherry from her. 'I really should be getting back to work. I can't go on just being a . . . a freeloader here when everyone else has a job to do. It makes me feel so useless.'

'You haven't heard any of us complain, have you?' Monica gave me a forgiving smile along with the sherry. I hadn't mentioned the body since Anderson's injection; she thought she was winning.

'You've all been wonderful.' I felt Ivor staring at me and tried not to notice. 'But I know I'm not pulling my weight. And the rest of you are so busy. I really would like to get back to work – or, at least, try to.'

'That might not be such a bad idea,' Monica said slowly. 'It could help get your mind off . . . your other problems. You might even start remembering things again, once you get back into the swing of your usual routine.'

The hostility was back. It struck me like a physical blow. I glanced around quickly, but couldn't pinpoint the source of it. Monica was still smiling at me, it seemed impossible that she hadn't felt it, too.

'Perhaps tomorrow,' a voice said behind me.

'Thank you, Shadow.' Monica beamed her smile over my shoulder.

I turned in time to see the man in black withdraw and

close the door. Shadow was a good name for him. My tensed muscles relaxed as I found I no longer felt the hatred that had lashed out at me so unexpectedly. I knew he didn't like me but . . .

'Shall we –?' Monica began, but the others were already moving towards the dining room. She shrugged at me and we fell in behind them.

Ivor was waiting for us. He gave me a self-satisfied smirk and nodded his head in approval. 'I think it will do you a world of good to come back to the office.'

I was immediately uneasy. If he was pleased, I must have done something wrong.

Whatever Nessa's real role had been in the Oversall scheme of things, it was obvious that I was not going to be allowed to step back into it. Not immediately. Not until I had proved myself.

'We thought we ought to start you off with something light.' Candy flashed that sharklike smile at me as she pulled out the chair at a desk almost buried under a mountain of blank envelopes.

'You won't remember, but Everett is such a stickler for propriety that he insists every Christmas card he sends must be hand-addressed.'

They must have decided that the Public Relations office was the best place to slot me into. I couldn't do any damage there. Except, perhaps, to myself.

'He certainly has a lot of friends.' I tried to keep the dismay out of my face. Not only were there all those envelopes covering the desktop, but further boxes were stacked beside and behind it.

Writer's cramp in waiting. I was glad I had taken the precaution of wearing the wrist support bandage.

'Oh, these are just for the worldwide staff,' Candy laughed. 'Every single employee in every one of his enter-prises gets a personal card from him. It's not just *public* relations we have to keep up to speed with. It's important to keep all our workers happy, too.'

How about the Poor Bloody Infantry they expected to address all those cards? This was the secretarial equivalent of being set to wash dishes in a busy restaurant. It was enough to drive a girl back to the chorus line.

Or to her own quarters with one of the headaches that seemed to be endemic around here. I was beginning to understand why.

'I'll have a go.' With a brave, game smile, I waggled my bandaged wrist in her face. 'But I don't know how well I'll do. I'm afraid I might be a bit slow.'

'There's no hurry. We always start early and the others will help out if you're overwhelmed.' Those teeth flashed again. 'Ivor's calligraphy is fantastic. And Nina can be quite good, too – when she puts her mind to it.'

That did it! I dropped into the chair and pulled the first stack of envelopes towards me.

'Take your time,' Candy cooed. 'When you get tired, or if your wrist starts aching, you can pack it in until tomorrow. We have plenty of time in hand.'

Maybe you have! My teeth might not be so sharp or white – or expensive – but I bared them at her anyway as I nodded.

'And if it *is* too much for you, you mustn't hesitate to tell me. You don't have to do it, you know. We're all quite happy to carry you for a while longer until you're fully recovered. The minute you're feeling tired, you must go and lie down. Everyone will understand.'

I'll bet they would! It was just what they wanted. Dear Nessa, frail and fragile – and safely out of the way.

I wouldn't give them the satisfaction. Grinding my teeth quietly, I settled down to work.

During the afternoon, I became aware that I was under fairly constant surveillance. People would appear in the doorway and look in on me, then disappear again.

I kept my head down and appeared too absorbed in my task to notice. At some point, a cup of tea materialized by my elbow, unsettling me. I hadn't heard anyone bring it in; I must have worked myself into a trance. And this was no place to let down my guard.

There was no biscuit with the tea and no milk or sugar in it. After a couple of sips, I abandoned the dark odd-flavoured brew. Perhaps it was herbal but, if I couldn't identify it, I wasn't going to drink it.

Candy spent most of her time on the telephone, talking in a firm cajoling voice about various projects under way and in the offing. People I had not seen before came and went. I realized there must be a substantial office force who came in by the day. More suspects? Or just innocent office staff carrying out their duties, forgetting everything when they clocked off at 5 p.m.?

They paid no attention to me, however, which made a refreshing change. No one claiming friendship, no one suggesting unspecified alliances, no one enquiring solicitously about my present state of health – everyone was completely indifferent to me. I was just another pair of hands around the office doing a menial job. Perhaps a temp, it was the sort of job they did.

Their behaviour also confirmed my suspicion that Nessa had not normally worked in this area of the building. I knew from her letters that she had an office of her own. It was obviously somewhere else. I intended to find it – if they'd let me.

On the plus side, I was in the Business Wing of the building, even though I had limited access to the more interesting parts of it.

I waited until Candy had a telephone call she seemed to be particularly involved in, then approached her desk with a slightly embarrassed air.

'I'm sorry,' I said as she looked up, 'but I'm afraid I haven't the faintest idea where the loo is. If you could give me directions –?'

'Just a moment,' she said. 'I'll show you.'

'No, no,' I protested. 'You're too busy. I don't want to interrupt. Just point me in the right direction. Or perhaps one of the girls could –'

'We'll talk later,' she said into the telephone and slammed it down impatiently, but rallied with a forbearing smile for me. 'Just come along, Nessa.'

It had been worth a try. I ground my teeth again as she led the way down a corridor and through several turnings. I managed to catch a glimpse into some of the rooms along the way before she stopped at a closed door.

'In here,' she said, opening it. 'I'll wait for you.'

'Oh, that won't be necessary. I'm sure I'll be able to find my own way back.'

'I'll wait.' She pulled the door closed behind me. At least she didn't try to come in with me. When I turned around, I could see why. It was a one-person place, a good-sized room that had been transformed into a disabled facility. Rather, one corner of it had been, as the appliance surrounded by strategically placed grab bars and the low-sited sink testified. The rest of the room was on the luxurious side, with a low dressing table complete with all accessories in sterling silver, a vase of fresh hothouse flowers and a bottle of mineral water. Beside another table was a motor-operated recliner and a reading lamp. The magazines on the table were the current issues of French, German, Spanish and Italian glossies, as well as their English counterparts. The soapdish by the sink held a bar of expensive French floral soap and fluffy Turkish towels were on the towel rack.

Above all, there was space; lots of uncluttered space, room for a wheelchair to move around in and turn easily.

It was clear that I was in Madame's private boudoir. I wondered if that wide door on the opposite side of the room opened into her own office. And whether she was occupying it –?

No luck. The knob turned, but the door didn't budge.

I stooped and tried the keyhole, but all I could see was the key in place on the other side of the lock.

'Nessa.' There was a sharp rapping on the door I had entered through. 'Nessa – are you all right?'

Damn! What was she doing – timing me?

'Yes, yes . . . coming.' I flushed the toilet ostentatiously and ran the hot water full force.

For good measure, I pinched my cheeks to get them suitably red, although sheer annoyance had given them a pink glow that could pass for embarrassment.

'Sorry,' I apologized. 'I . . . I was feeling a bit dizzy and had to sit down for a minute.'

'It's all right. I didn't mean to rush you,' Candy said, although the pace at which she was striding back to her office said otherwise. 'Perhaps you've done enough for today. We don't want to knock you out your first day back.' Again, her tone suggested that that was just what she would like to do.

'Perhaps I *should* take time for a nap before dinner,' I agreed.

'You could have dinner in your room –'

'Oh, no, I'll be quite all right after a nap. I must get back into the proper routine. It will be good for me.'

'I suppose so,' she said reluctantly.

'On the other hand . . .' I decided to change my mind. The thought of the long evening dragging out after dinner gave me pause. Also, I had already decided that there might be more to learn in the Business Wing than in the dining room.

'Perhaps it *would* be a good idea if I had an early night after all this exertion. Then I'll be nice and fresh to face those envelopes in the morning.'

'If you're sure you're feeling strong enough to carry on with them . . .'

Why did I get the impression that she didn't really want me hanging around her office, that she had drawn the short straw when it came to keeping me occupied, but sidelined?

'Oh, I will be,' I assured her blithely. 'I'm just aching to get on with the job. You can depend on me.'

'Oh, good,' she said, with a noticeable lack of enthusiasm.

Chapter Seventeen

'Where the hell have you been?' It was nearly midnight and the message Anderson had smuggled to me had implied that he'd be earlier than that. I snatched his arm and yanked him inside, banged the door shut and slammed him up against it.

'Tut-tut, you've been reading your private eye books again . . . Nessa.' He rubbed his arm ruefully. 'However would you explain it if anyone had seen you?'

'Never mind being cute! They didn't. There's no one around to see anything.'

'Then perhaps I should only talk to you when there are witnesses around.' He rubbed harder and winced. 'It might be safer.'

'Don't worry, you're perfectly safe.' He must be feeling more relaxed with me, if he could begin to make jokes. Either that or –

'How is she?' I demanded.

'I think – I don't want to raise any false hopes –' his face brightened, he almost smiled – 'but I think she's going to make it.'

'Thank God!' I slumped into a chair.

'We're a long way from out of the woods yet,' he warned. 'And I can't guarantee just what the . . . the residual damage . . . might be.'

'She'll live.'

'Possibly . . . probably . . . but . . .'

'But what?' I fought against the knowledge he was trying to impart. 'That's enough. For now.'

'Exactly,' he said. 'For now. As for the future –' He shrugged. 'I suppose what I really want to say is that one option is closed to us now.'

'Option?' This was the first I'd heard of there being any. 'What option?'

'Er . . .' He didn't want to tell me. He avoided my eyes.

'What option?' If I had to force it out of him, I would.

'Well . . . we don't have to make the choice about pulling the plug. She's functioning on her own now.'

'Pull the plug?' He was right not to want to say it. I nearly hit him. I wanted to kill him for even thinking such a thing. 'That was never an option!'

'Immaterial now.' He shrugged. 'In fact, we took her off the machine yesterday and she's doing fine on her own.'

'You took her off? Without consulting me? You had no right to do any such thing! I'm the next of kin!'

'And I'm the medical expert.' He said it as though he could convince me, but he took a prudent step backwards. I vaguely noticed that the cat had disappeared completely.

'How expert? Have you ever had a case like hers before?'

'Not exactly like hers, but we've had some pretty grim cases flown in from the oil rigs. You get to have a feeling about these things.'

'A feeling! You risked Nessa's life because you had a feeling!'

'I was right.' He backed another step. 'It had to be done sometime.'

'Without consulting her next of kin!'

'Save your energy. The hard part is still to come. If she recovers consciousness –'

'*If?*'

'If she comes out of the coma,' he continued firmly, 'we'll be able to assess the damage, see what can be done to repair it, find out what she needs for rehabilitation, all of that and perhaps more. Don't worry.' His mouth twisted wryly. 'We'll have plenty of consultations in the days ahead.'

'We'd better!' I shook my head. 'I can't believe it! You did something that dangerous without even talking to her next of kin! You ignored me –'

'We were both busy – and I was afraid you'd react like this. I didn't want you to blow your cover in an unguarded moment.'

'Very thoughtful of you. I wonder if the Medical Council would consider that a sufficient excuse.'

'You wouldn't –' He paled.

'I might.' But I was in no position to do any such thing at the moment and we both knew it, I realized, as his colour began to return. 'If it ever happens again. Meanwhile, I'd suggest you brush up on your medical ethics.'

'Don't worry –' Was he bold enough now to have a trace of mockery in his tone? 'I'll make very sure the next of kin is kept fully informed from now on.'

'See that you do.' But I couldn't antagonize him too much; he was my lifeline to Nessa. And there was another point he could satisfy my curiosity about.

'Everett Oversall –' There was no subtle way to segue into the subject, so I plunged in without preliminaries. 'I haven't seen him yet. I've heard of keeping a low profile, but this is ridiculous. I'm beginning to wonder if he still exists.'

'Oh, he exists, all right. Never doubt it. And he's an expert at ensuring that he'll continue to exist.'

'What do you mean by that?' The mockery in his voice had shaded into an interesting bitterness that hinted at volumes that could be spoken.

'Haven't you found out yet?' It was unmistakably a taunt, possibly a dare.

'Suppose you tell me.'

'Suppose I don't.' He was paying me back for the threat to report him to the General Medical Council. I'd have liked to do more than that to him!

Careful. Keep calm. Much as I'd have liked to ram his teeth down his throat, it was out-of-character for Vanessa and would be hard to explain. Apart from which, she

132

wouldn't thank me if she recovered to find herself facing a charge of grievous bodily harm.

'Spit it out! This isn't a personal favour to me, you know. It's for Nessa.'

'Nessa . . . yes . . .' His mood changed. He looked at me with a strange expression of aversion and . . .? 'Nessa . . . She should have got away while there was still time.'

'The way Francesca did?'

'Perhaps. Sometimes I wonder . . .' His gaze sharpened. 'At least you found out about *her*, did you?'

'You were going to tell me,' I reminded him, 'what else I should have found out.'

'Was I?' He looked around, as though searching for escape, and was momentarily distracted by the cat who had sauntered back into the room now that our voices were quieter, afraid of missing something.

'Here, girl . . .' He snapped his fingers at her, but she went into full Grand Duchess mode and sat down at a distance, staring at him coldly.

We both stared at him, coldly and silently, until the silence was abruptly shattered.

'Good God!' He jumped visibly and looked towards the cloister. 'What's that?'

That was a blurred melodic chanting sounding faintly in the distance somewhere along the cloister.

'Just one of my hallucinations. Pay no attention.' Either someone wasn't aware that I had company, or they knew and didn't care because they knew who it was – a witness who could be controlled.

'You . . . you've heard it before?'

'It's getting to be a regular nightly concert. That's the reason I didn't sleep so well last night and am a bit snappy today.' It was as close as I was going to get to an apology.

'What the hell is going on?' It was tacitly accepted and we were back on an even footing.

'Who knows?' I shrugged. 'I suspect it's intended to

make me rush outside in girlish excitement to try to find out. But I don't happen to think that's a good idea.'

'Do you think that's what Nessa did?'

'And, possibly, even Francesca.'

'Yes . . .' He considered that for a moment. 'Yes, Francesca was the excitable type. I could see her doing that. But I'm not so sure about Nessa.'

'It might have taken more to smoke her out,' I agreed. 'But – why should anyone want to? And what about the woman I saw in the anchorite's cell? Who was she? Anyone we know?'

'I'm sorry about that injection.' It was his turn to apologize. 'In the circumstances, it was the only thing I could do – and it was only half-strength, you know.'

'I appreciate that.' Apology accepted, but deed not quite forgiven. And he still hadn't answered the question.

In the distance, that chanting ratcheted up a notch. Now there seemed to be an organ accompaniment.

'I don't believe this!' Anderson shook his head groggily. 'What the hell is going on?'

'I believe they're trying to drive Nessa mad,' I told him. 'Or else convince other people that she already *is* mad. That's why I haven't mentioned this to any of them.'

The cat stalked over to the door, tail lashing. She was furious. She'd had enough! She glared over her shoulder at us and her message was clear: *Do* something about it!

'The cat can hear it, too.' Anderson sounded as though her evidence was more reliable than his own ears. I knew the feeling. 'What are you going to do?'

'Nothing. That's what someone wants – me rushing out impulsively. Straight into whatever they've got waiting for me out there.'

'I could –' he began.

'Don't even think of it!' I cut him off. 'Their plan would probably work just as well if they killed you – and blamed Nessa for it. Perhaps even better. They could pin the other killing on her, too.'

'*Other?* But she wasn't even here when Francesca –' He broke off, abruptly realizing he'd gone too far.

'Who said anything about Francesca? I'm talking about the body in the cell.'

'Look – I told you the truth about that. Monica took me to it to see for myself. There was no body in the cell. Nothing but the effigy of the monk – just as there's always been.'

'We'll come back to that later.' He'd started to rise, but I pushed him back into the chair. 'First, try telling me the truth about Francesca.'

'I don't know anything about Francesca.' He folded his arms across his chest and looked at me defiantly.

I clenched my fist, then unclenched it, fighting for control. If what I suspected was true, this might be my future brother-in-law. If I didn't kill him first.

'Then tell me more about what you don't know.'

'She . . . left . . . so suddenly.' He was desperately unhappy at admitting anything. His gaze slithered from me to the cat, to the door, back to me. 'Everyone was saying she'd eloped, but . . .'

'But you don't quite believe that, do you?'

'I . . . don't know . . . I'm not sure . . .' He looked at the door again, but both the cat and I stood between him and it.

'The Elopement?' I prodded. 'Or the Disappearance? Forget what you don't know, what do you suspect? And why?'

'The Golden Handcuffs,' he said. 'I don't think she'd risk losing those. She was too close to collecting.'

'Golden Handcuffs?' I didn't like the sound of that. 'What do you mean?'

'You've got them, too. That is, Nessa has. All of the women have. Why do you think they bury themselves in a place like this and put up with all of Oversall's whims?'

'I've wondered. But I thought he was running some sort

135

of Home for Retired Mistresses – and paying over the odds in memory of old times.'

'Close . . . but not quite on target.'

'Except for Nessa, of course,' I qualified hastily.

'Of course.' Now that he'd admitted that much, he was ready to talk more – if not tell all. 'He pays well, but not that well, although the board and lodging count for a good bit, but the real perk is the bonus system. The Golden Handcuffs is the name they give it among themselves because that's the way it works. The longer you stay in his employment, the richer in your own right you become.'

So that was why Madame thought I was greedy. To the point of being reckless with my own life. Nessa's life.

'Explain,' I said. 'Just how *does* it work?'

'Extremely well. Oversall has gifted each one with a very substantial sum, set up in a trust fund which they will have access to after seven years. Neither he nor they have to pay tax on it – provided that he lives for seven years after the gift. He repeats this with fresh funds every seven years. Needless to say, they take very good care of him. They're not just part of the entertainment when he has some of his dodgy business associates calling on him. They're the best bodyguard available – they have a vested interest in his continuing good health. I believe Yvonne actually did save his life on one occasion when she spotted a Dictator's apprentice unsheathing a concealed knife too close to Oversall's back. And Amanda is a genius at sussing out anyone high on drugs or otherwise mentally unstable. Those two are better guard dogs than any of the four-legged variety patrolling the grounds.'

'Does this just apply to the women?' I thought of Ivor – was he out of the arrangements and angling for a wealthy wife? 'Or do the men benefit, too?'

'Actually, they do.' His face crimsoned; he thought I was getting at him. '*We* do.'

'So you all do double duty. Along with your nominal jobs, you're part of his private army.'

'If you want to put it like that, yes.'

136

'I'd say it was a fair assessment of the situation. So, with all this money in the offing, if Francesca eloped, it would have to be with a multimillionaire to make it worth her while?'

'Precisely – and there weren't any around at the time she disappeared. In fact, Oversall had no visitors at all that week. He spent it closeted with the auditors – and none of them had enough of an income to be of interest to Francesca.'

'Interesting . . .' It was even more interesting that neither of us considered her being swept away by love as a possibility.

'Interesting . . . and disturbing.'

'If Nessa was enrolled in this private army, then I'm even more surprised that Oversall hasn't sent for me yet. Doesn't he object to the fact that I'm not pulling my full weight along with the rest?'

'He's a realist above all. He knows you're not much use to him at the moment. He'll bide his time.' Anderson glared at me briefly before looking towards the cloister. 'That music has stopped.'

The cat looked in that direction, too, then her ears flattened and she streaked for the bedroom. The music may have stopped, but something else was happening.

'Perhaps –' Anderson stood and I made no move to stop him – 'this would be a good moment for me to get away. I'll take a look around outside before I leave,' he added placatingly.

'Don't bother.' Now I could hear what the cat had heard. 'It's being taken care of.'

'What –?'

'Miss Nessa?' There was a light tap on the door. 'You all right in there?' A soft *'Woof?'* echoed the enquiry.

'It's Bud,' I said. 'Making his rounds. He'll see you to your car.'

'I don't need –'

But I had already crossed to the door and opened it,

not wide enough to let Brutus in, although he shoved forward.

'Dr Anderson was just leaving, Bud. Perhaps you'd be kind enough to take him to his car,' I said, as Bud stepped aside to let Anderson out.

'What's the doctor doing here?' Bud glared at Anderson suspiciously. 'You all right?'

'She's fine,' Anderson said. 'I'm just making sure she stays that way.'

'He giving you any trouble?' Bud hung back to ask with quiet menace.

'No, no, it's all right. He's fine.' Bud's sudden protectiveness made me nervous. Annoying though he was, I didn't want any accident to happen to Anderson on the way to his car. 'Everything is fine.'

'Right, then.' He hovered uncertainly, not sure whether to believe me or not.

I smiled at him reassuringly.

'Right.' He leaned towards me and lowered his voice. 'Anyone bothers you, just let me know. I'll take care of them.'

Brutus growled agreement.

Chapter Eighteen

By mid-morning, the other office staff were getting used to having me around.

One of the townies brought a cup of coffee and set it down beside a pile of envelopes with the sympathetic smile of one who was awfully glad that she hadn't been lumbered with that miserable dead-end job.

Later, I became aware of someone standing by my elbow and looked up to find Yvonne staring down at me pensively.

'It is so good to see you back . . . at work,' she said.

Back where you belong, she had almost said. But this was not where I belonged and we both knew it, although she didn't know that I knew it.

'Thank you,' I smiled. This was the first time she had ever put herself out to be friendly. I waited for the ulterior motive to surface.

'Is it beginning to seem familiar?' The solicitous voice on my other side made me jump. I hadn't been aware that anyone was standing there.

'Sorry, I didn't mean to startle you,' Amanda said. She and Yvonne exchanged glances over my head. 'I was just wondering if all this was bringing back any memories.'

'None at all, I'm afraid.' The admission didn't seem to cheer them particularly, perhaps because there had never been any memories to connect with this job or this office. 'But it's good to be doing something useful again.' I gave them a brave smile.

'Yes, well, keep up the good work.' For a moment, it

looked as though Amanda was going to pat me on the shoulder, but she restrained herself and settled for a nod instead. Yvonne was already moving away.

Bemused, I drew another stack of envelopes towards me and went on with the addressing as though nothing unusual had happened. But this was the first time either of them had paid any attention to me. They had remained aloof while the others had tried to claim friendship or intimacy. Interesting . . . to find them now suddenly prepared to be chummy. Was it because I had been no threat to them before – but was now impinging on their territory?

A room I had never seen before (no surprise there) functioned as the Staff Canteen. I arrived late, hoping the corridors might be deserted enough to allow for some exploration, under the guise of having lost my way. I had already suspected that none of the senior staff would use the place and I was right. No one questioned my being there, however.

The unfriendly maid was behind the food counter, which was fine; I wasn't in the mood for cheerful greetings. The most popular item on the menu seemed to have been the pork-and-leek sausages, there were only a few left. I nodded towards them and added a portion of onion mash and grilled tomatoes. I wouldn't have minded a side order of the macaroni-and-cheese, but I was supposed to have a ladylike appetite.

Murmuring my thanks, I carried my tray over to a table at the end of the room and took a seat with my back to the wall. I could see everything that was going on and no one could sneak up on me. Almost immediately, this proved to be a wise move.

I saw him coming. I snatched up my tray and stood, but it was too late, he was faster. He stood at the end of the table, blocking my exit, then moved closer, invading my space. Smiling that oily smile, almost drooling.

'*Dear* Vanessa –' Ivor smirked. 'I thought I might find you here.' He moved closer, forcing me to inch back. The only alternative would be to hurl the contents of my tray in his face and, tempting though the idea was, there were too many interested faces turned in our direction.

'And how does it feel to be back at work?' He set down his tray, he had the macaroni-and-cheese and nothing else. 'Are you settling in well? Are you enjoying it? Are you . . . remembering . . . the old days?' He rolled his eyes insinuatingly at me and took the seat opposite, stretching out his legs so that I would fall over them if I made a dash for freedom. He behaved like a man with a lot of experience in herding unwilling sheep into places they didn't want to go.

But I wasn't the ewe he thought I was. On the other hand, I was going to have to deal with him sooner or later, and this might be the best place to make a start. In full view of a lot of interested eavesdroppers who could only guess at the undercurrents.

'I'm all right.' I reset my own tray on the table and sat down again, looking around for possible allies.

I encountered a couple of sympathetic smiles and a hostile glare from behind the counter. Charm Girl didn't like any of us, but she disliked Ivor even more than most. I couldn't fault her for that.

'You're looking better. Quite blooming, in fact.'

'I still haven't remembered anything.' I cut short the phoney compliments. 'Not one teeny thing.'

'What a shame,' his voice said. *Jackpot!* his expression said. 'How disappointed you must be.'

'Not that much. They warned me I might never . . .' I let my voice quaver . . . 'never get my past life back.'

'You must let me help you, my dear. I can tell you what we used to do –' He reached for my hand. 'I can *show* you what we used to do.'

'Not now!' I stabbed one of my sausages with a savagery that made him wince and recoil swiftly. His instinct was right. It was only at the last moment that I had diverted my fork from his groping hand. *Never, never, never* had Nessa had anything to do with this clown!

'Perhaps you're right.' He looked around, smirking. 'This isn't the time or place. We must reminisce in private.'

On a freezing day in hell! Nothing he told me would ever be true. Was he as obvious as he looked? Was he just trying to take over a vulnerable young woman he otherwise would never have stood a chance with? Or did he have another, more sinister, agenda? With a feeling of deep depression, I knew that I was going to have to find out.

'We can talk later,' I said reluctantly. '*Much* later.'

'Not *that* much later.' He pushed away his untouched food and got to his feet. 'I'll be –' that insinuating plummy note slid back into his voice as he ogled me complacently – '*in touch.*'

He walked away with a self-satisfied strut. My gloom lifted slightly as I had a cheering thought: if he got too obnoxious, Bud would be more than willing to sort him out.

I lingered over my coffee until even the unfriendly server gave up, dismantled her hot table and went away after telling me, with a poisonous look, to leave the dirty cup on the counter, she'd deal with it later.

The corridor was deserted when I finally left. Looking both ways to be sure, I moved off in the opposite direction to the way I had arrived. If anyone challenged me, I was lost and looking for the way back.

All the doors along this route were firmly closed, no sound to be heard from behind them. The corridor twisted and became narrower, the lighting seemed dimmer. Perhaps this wing was unused.

The flagstone path leading off from the next turning was so narrow and dark that I nearly missed it. It could have been some medieval twitten running between two dwellings, except for the roof above it and the door it led up to.

I tried the door cautiously and it swung open on well-oiled hinges. The carpet beyond was deep and luxurious, the wall sconces glowed warm and welcoming. This part of the building was definitely inhabited. It felt more like a private home than any place I had yet encountered.

Intrigued but wary, I moved forward, trying to look unaware that I was trespassing. I had not been invited into these superior quarters.

Somewhere ahead, familiar piano music rippled through the air. Yvonne. Was this her private apartment? I didn't want to run into her but, as long as the music kept playing, that was unlikely.

In any case, I had covered too much distance to retrace my steps now. It was safer to go forward and trust the carpet to muffle all sound as I hurried past her door. There were other doors beyond hers, one of them must lead me out of this maze.

I headed towards the most promising, the one straight ahead with the corridor dividing into two paths in front of it. With luck, it might open into the grounds and I could –

The music stopped abruptly, followed by a crash, as of a keyboard lid being slammed down. The recital was over, the pianist was not in a good mood.

The last thing I wanted to do was to encounter her. I was supposed to be at my desk addressing those stupid envelopes. She would not be pleased to find me here.

I turned and, walking backwards, kept my eye on Yvonne's door. Perhaps she was just tired of the piano and was going to settle down with a magazine or something.

The door began to open. I swung around and bolted for cover. The door straight ahead was already slightly ajar and no indication of life came from the room behind it. I dashed inside and closed the door silently before turning to face the room.

Out of the frying pan . . .

I'd wanted to see Everett Oversall – but not this way.

The Great Man sat behind a large gleaming mahogany desk, facing the door. A blonde head bent close to his, hair almost sweeping his cheek as she shuffled documents for him to sign, not noticing that she had lost his attention.

I had it.

Caught in the laser beam from his eyes like a rabbit paralysed by oncoming headlights, I could only blink. And blink again, my mind gone blank.

'Come in . . . Vanessa,' he said.

'What?' Amanda's head snapped back. 'What are you doing here?' Now I was caught in two laser beams. 'How did you get in?'

'I lost my way,' I said feebly. 'Where am I?'

'Home,' Oversall said. Those hooded eyes seemed to bore into me and I stared back helplessly. He was smaller than I had expected, in the way celebrities and film stars are always smaller in real life than they look in pictures and on film. Perhaps he was shrinking with age, but he still exuded an aura of power.

'You've found your way home.' He gave a short bark that might have been intended as laughter. 'It didn't take you as long as I thought it might.'

'Lost?' Amanda was not so amused. 'A likely story! You've remembered, haven't you? You thought you'd sneak in here and –'

'Amanda!' Oversall cut her off sharply. A quick look passed between them.

'I don't remember anything,' I protested. 'I wish I could. This . . . this is all so awful!'

Everett Oversall had kept both hands on his desk, toying with a ruby-tipped fountain pen, surely a gift from some Middle Eastern potentate. You don't find writing instruments that florid in your local branch of Ryman's.

So, when the door flew open and Yvonne burst into the room, I knew it must have been Amanda who had hit the panic button.

'What is *she* doing here?' Yvonne demanded as she saw me.

144

'Remembering, I think.' Amanda met her eyes. 'If not now, then soon.'

And why should that bother them so much?

'If only I *could* remember,' I said. 'I keep trying – but there's nothing there.' Tears would be excessive, I decided, but I allowed my voice to quaver. 'Nothing at all!'

'You poor dear.' Yvonne's sympathy was as false as her eyelashes. 'We must take you back to your rooms where you can rest.'

'Yes.' Amanda closed in on me from the other side. 'You need to lie down and sleep. This is all too much for you.'

Hands like iron bands snapped around my wrists on either side, and they turned me relentlessly towards the door.

'Just a minute.' Everett Oversall intervened before they could lead me away. 'If there's a chance she might remember some of her past by being here, I think it's a chance worth taking.' His mouth stretched in a semblance of a smile. 'After all, we want our Vanessa back again, don't we?'

In the instant before they rearranged them into agreement, their frozen faces said they didn't want Vanessa back, they didn't want the other women who were cluttering up the place – and they could do without each other, too.

'Yes –' I twisted my arms suddenly, breaking free of their grip. 'Yes, that might help. It's worth trying.'

'I'd hoped you'd think so.' His eyes met mine grimly before flicking away to indicate a door on the far side of the room. I had the disconcerting feeling that I had just been sent a subliminal instruction.

It was obviously the only clue I was going to get, so I followed it – not forgetting to rub my wrists with an accusing look towards the ladies so anxious to get me out of there.

I began to wander around the opulent office, aware of

Oversall's almost imperceptible nod of approval as I started off in the opposite direction, peering vaguely into shadowy corners and pausing to admire paintings.

When I finally reached the door he had indicated and put my hand on the knob, tension flashed through the room behind me like a bolt of lightning.

Without looking back, I opened the door and stepped inside. I heard a muffled gasp as I switched on the lights – but most light switches were just inside the door; that didn't prove my memory was returning.

It was a warm and inviting room, the deep blue of the blue-and-silver-grey carpet matched by the window curtains, a polished rosewood desk glowing, logs waiting to be ignited in the fireplace, more paintings, a bookcase filled with tempting volumes – and a faint nostalgic fragrance in the air.

And not one damned envelope in sight.

I had found Vanessa's domain. I knew it even before I saw the parade of foreign souvenirs trailing across the mantelpiece – every one of them sent to her from me on my travels.

I had picked up the paperweight of the pyramids and upended it to start the unlikely snowstorm fluttering down when I became aware that they were all standing in the doorway watching me.

'Oh . . .' I replaced the paperweight, the swirling snow now almost completely obscuring the pyramids. I'd thought it would amuse Vanessa and it had. But there was nothing funny about it now, nor about anything else.

'Oh . . .' I turned to face them; the tears blurring my eyes were genuine, they weren't to know the true cause. 'I thought . . . just for a moment . . . but it's gone again. It's . . . all gone . . .'

'Sleep!' Amanda started towards me purposefully. 'That's what you need. A good night's sleep. I have some pills, if you don't –'

'She must rest,' Yvonne concurred. 'She is still weak and frail.' She moved forward. 'Come now, you need –'

'That's enough!' Oversall's raised hand stopped them in their tracks. 'I've rung for Monica. She'll be here in a minute – and she'll take care of Vanessa.'

So he didn't really trust them, either.

Chapter Nineteen

The phone rang before I had dressed for work in the morning. Half-expecting Anderson, I was surprised to find it was Candy with my marching, or rather, non-marching orders for the day.

'There's another dreary crisis this morning,' she said. 'There's nothing you can do about it and the rest of us are going to be frantically busy sorting it out, so it might be better if you just skipped work today.'

Keep out from underfoot, I translated.

'You're sure there's nothing I can do to help?' I made the obligatory offer to show willing.

'It's all in hand. Just a matter of tracing and finding some publicity material that went missing on its way to various media people. It happens every now and again. We have dealing with it down to a fine art – but it's hectic here while we do. We'll have it all sorted out by tomorrow.'

We don't want you in the way today.

'Well, if you're sure I can't –'

'Consider it a day's holiday. Of course –' her tone became arch, signalling a joke – 'if you're really determined to work, we can always send some envelopes over!'

'Thanks, but no thanks.' I gave the expected little laugh. 'Actually –' I fell back on what seemed to be the standard excuse around here – 'I have a bit of a headache. Not to mention a touch of writer's cramp. I'd appreciate the chance to catch up on my rest.'

'That's settled then.' She was pleased. Had she expected more of a protest? 'You just take it easy today. You've worked so hard you deserve a day off. See you in the morning.' She rang off.

In the morning? Which one of us wasn't expected at dinner tonight?

As for the rest of the day: *take it easy* – *Hah!* I had my full maintenance routine to catch up with.

I slept so late the next morning that I found my fruit and muesli breakfast tray had been joined by another tray filled with a well-wrapped and extensive selection of sandwiches – a clear indication that I was not expected to appear in the Staff Canteen for lunch.

I considered what might happen if I were to appear in Everett Oversall's office instead. The idea was tempting, but I was fairly certain that I would be intercepted before I got anywhere near Oversall. They would be expecting a move like that. But there were more promising leads I wanted to investigate first.

I poured the milk into the muesli and the coffee cream into the cat's bowl. Then, in response to her imperious look, I prised apart some of the dainty crustless triangles that had been supplied for lunch and, perhaps, dinner.

The cat had been in a strange mood earlier, but was happily grazing through the prawn cocktail, egg-and-cress, roast beef, tuna-and-sweetcorn, and chicken salad by the time I was ready to leave.

'I'm just popping round to see Madame.' For a moment, I felt this proved they were succeeding in driving me mad. Discussing my plans with the cat like that.

But she raised her head and gave me what seemed to be an approving look as she clawed aside an almost transparent slice of cucumber to get at the smoked salmon beneath it, leaving me to wonder whether she had actually understood what I had told her.

'I shouldn't be long.' I slipped out and locked the door securely behind me.

The late afternoon was mild, but damp, grey and foggy. Not actually raining – that was a bonus. I had almost reached Madame's cottage when I realized I was being followed.

Not very subtly, either. There was a rustling, brushing noise behind me. I turned to find a dispirited peacock dragging his folded clump of tail feathers along the path. He stared at me bleakly, waiting to see what I was going to do.

'You must be Petruchio.' It was an easy guess; he had made no move to challenge me, as Percy would have done. He hadn't been very aptly named.

'What's the matter, fella? Life getting you down?' Then I heard why.

'Petruchio . . .? Petruchio . . .?' Nina's voice called seductively. 'Where are you?'

I nearly tripped over him as we both dived for the shelter of the boxwood hedge. Once we were cowering behind it, he shot me a look of unmistakable complicity. We were companions in adversity.

'Petruchio . . .? Where are you?' Footsteps crunched past on the gravel path. 'I have a lovely handful of corn for you . . . Come to Nina.'

Not bloody likely! We hunched down until the footsteps and the insistent voice faded away.

'That was close.' I was talking to the fauna again, but no longer felt awkward about it as he blinked in distinct agreement before creeping back on to the path and heading in the opposite direction.

'Mind how you go,' I advised. 'And if I run into her, I'll keep her busy until you have time to get clear.'

Another acknowledging blink and he made off through the shrubbery and vanished.

Being in no hurry to encounter Nina myself, I slowed down and kept a wary lookout.

The path ahead was clear; no sight nor sound of Nina. Nor of anyone else. Good.

Then the hairs on the back of my neck prickled and I froze halfway down the path to the cottage as the faint strains of music reached my ears.

But it was all right. Nothing monkish, not even vaguely liturgical. I started forward again. Just a good honest classical concerto, soothing background music for an afternoon nap, perhaps. I hoped Madame wouldn't be in too bad a mood if I disturbed her.

I tapped on the door and it swung open. I hesitated only a moment before stepping inside; it wouldn't do to be caught lurking on the doorstep.

This time I was willing to follow the music – into the dark parlour where Madame lay motionless on her chaise longue, a cashmere throw covering her.

Was she too still? I could discern no sign of breathing. The sense of desolation that swept over me surprised me. It was not just that she might have taken the key to Nessa's life here with her – I had been growing genuinely fond of the old girl.

I stood there, indecisive and helpless, looking down at her. Should I charge through the cottage shouting for Richie? Should I ring Monica and tell her to call Anderson? Should I –?

I became aware that her eyes had opened and she was staring back at me.

'So, Vanessa,' she breathed. 'I have been expecting you. You are late.'

'Are you all right?' I asked. 'Really all right?'

'Why should I not be?' She was irritated. 'What do you think I –?'

'Madame –' I knelt beside her, my face close to hers. She almost smiled.

'Ah, yes, we are Old Souls, you and I, Vanessa. Older than Lilith . . . older than Cain . . .'

'Madame –?' Was she rambling? That was all I needed.

'What the hell are *you* doing here?' Richie was back – if he had ever been away.

'She gets in everywhere!' Shadow was with him, staring at me with utter loathing.

Nessa, Nessa, what did you ever do to him?

'Madame is too tired for visitors today,' Richie said. 'You'd better leave.'

'I will decide –' Madame began.

'*Now!*' Richie was at my side, looming over me ominously.

I stumbled to my feet before he could drag me to them ignominiously.

'I'll take her back where she belongs.' Shadow was glowering at me, he looked as though he'd enjoy yanking me to the door and frogmarching me out of there.

Whatever happened to chivalry?

'Vanessa is my guest –' Madame tried again, but she was outnumbered. Against Richie or Shadow alone, she might have prevailed, but united they were going to win.

For the moment, the dangerous flash of her eyes threatened.

'This isn't one of your better days,' Richie insisted.

'Vanessa has other things to do right now.' Shadow crowded closer, one hand reaching out for my upper arm. A grim satisfaction appeared in his eyes as I shrank away.

He thought I was afraid of him. He wasn't to know it was because I didn't want that domineering hand to discover a stronger muscular structure than Nessa possessed.

'Another time, Vanessa,' Madame promised. 'We will speak again – when there is no one to disturb us.'

'That's right, Madame.' Richie gently rearranged her cashmere throw. 'Plenty of time. Vanessa will come again.'

But not if they had anything to say about it. I could almost hear the clang of iron bars closing around Madame.

'Come on!' Shadow opened the door and crowded me through, not quite touching me, but with his constant slow advance forcing me forward to avoid it.

'Shouldn't you be looking after Mr Overall?' I snapped.

'There's more than one way of looking after him,' he said. Keeping me out of the way was clearly one of them.

'Why don't you like me?' I didn't expect an honest answer, but it was worth trying.

'Why should I? Does everyone have to like you?'

'It would help.'

'So you think you need help, do you?' He edged closer. I moved away. 'You may be right.'

The sudden darkness of the long grey November night had engulfed the world while I was in the cottage. There were no lights along the paths. In the distance, I heard a dog bark.

How long would it take Bud to get here if I screamed?

'Do I? I don't know.' I kept my voice even, but increased speed. Unobtrusively, I hoped. 'I can't remember anything.'

'No?' He was disbelieving. 'You think you're so bloody clever! You –' He broke off, choking on his hatred.

The far end of the cloister was just discernible. I broke into a sprint, hauling up the hem of the kaftan and without looking back. I didn't know what Shadow's problem was, but he wasn't going to take it out on me. Not here, not now, in the darkness with no witnesses.

'Damn you!' He caught up with me at the cell. For a moment he pinned me against the bars. Neither of us gave even a fleeting glance inside.

'Pushing your way in here! Sneaking around where you're not wanted! Get out! Go back where you came from!'

'I might,' I said. 'If I could remember where that was.'

'You –!' His face, mottled with a rage that was almost out of control, was too close to mine. His hand swung out

to slap, then clenched into a fist, then fell to his side.
'You –! Mother –'

I waited for the remaining two syllables, trying to decide
whether I should register shock, outrage or disdain.

In the event, they didn't come. He looked beyond me,
bit down on what he had been going to say, and moved
back.

'Just go!' he snarled. 'Anywhere! Leave! Disappear!' He
stepped farther back and followed his own advice.
Abruptly, he was gone.

I turned to walk the remaining length of the cloister and
saw why Shadow had left so suddenly. There was a witness waiting at my door, watching my approach. My
unlikely saviour.

Caught between the devil and the deep blue sea.

Not that the most optimistic would call Ivor deep, but he
was marginally better than Shadow. At least I had some
inkling of what he wanted.

He watched me for a long moment before obviously
deciding that it would be politic to come to meet me. Or
perhaps he was afraid I might get away.

'I was beginning to think you weren't home,' he said.

'I wasn't.'

'But you are now.' He watched greedily as I unlocked
the door and moved in closer. I wasn't going to get an
opportunity to slip inside and close the door in his face.

'And now we can have our little talk,' he said.

Must we? But I had to do it sometime and the events of
the day so far had put me in a nasty mood. Just right for
dealing with Ivor. Silently, I allowed him to follow me
inside.

The cat came to greet me, took one look at Ivor and
walked away again. *I know the feeling, Duchess.*

'There's something different about this place,' he
declared, looking around. That ham-actor note was back in
his voice. 'Now, what can it be?'

'Everything is just the way it was when I got back from
the hospital,' I said.

'No. No . . . something's missing.' He frowned.

I waited.

'I know!' He tried to look triumphant, but succeeded in looking shifty. 'You used to have a big silver-framed picture of me on your desk.'

'Really?' *The hell I had.*

'Perhaps someone tidied it away while you were gone. Put it in one of the drawers . . .' But the drawer he started to open was much too small to contain a framed picture – it had obviously been intended for stamps and sealing wax.

'There's no picture in there!' I reached over and slammed the drawer shut before he had it fully open. 'There's no picture of you anywhere here. Believe me, I'd have noticed.'

'Of course you would.' He smirked, taking it as a compliment. 'Never mind, I'll give you another.'

'Don't bother!' He was getting on my nerves even more than usual. I certainly didn't want any reminders of him when he wasn't actually present – and I was sure Nessa didn't, either.

'Oh, it's no bother.' He tried to move closer, but I moved first and settled myself in the armchair farthest from the sofa, leaving that for him.

'Why don't you come and sit over here?' He patted the place beside him in what he seemed to consider an inviting manner.

'I'm fine here.' It was an offer easy to refuse.

'But we always used to sit together here,' he pouted. 'With the lights low . . . It might help you to remember.'

'Sorry, but I'm afraid you're still a complete stranger to me. I don't even know what you do around here.'

'Ah, well . . . I don't want to boast but . . .' He shot a glance at me to see how I was taking this outbreak of modesty.

With about a kilo of salt. 'But . . .?' I encouraged.

'You might call me a talent scout. I maintain an overview of everyone coming up in our various fields of interest and

155

work to acquire the brightest and best candidates for positions we have open.' He spoke too glibly and avoided my eyes.

'And does that entail hiring them away from other firms?' I was beginning to get the picture: it was the purest form of industrial espionage. No creeping around photocopying secret formulas or hacking into rival computer files, just hire one of the head honchos away from your competitor and he'll arrive quite legally with all the relevant information stored in his brain.

'Possibly . . . occasionally . . . if necessary . . .' He sent me a melting look. 'You're one of my notable successes, you know. In more ways than one.'

'Really?' I ignored the insinuation. 'Where did you hire me from?'

'Quite an important firm of financial advisers – the name would mean nothing to you . . . the way you are now.'

And obviously the way I was expected to remain – if he thought he could get away with that. Nessa's last job had been designing costumes for a new production of *Love's Labour's Lost*. How she had moved from there to here, I didn't know, but I was quite sure that Ivor had had nothing to do with it.

'We grew close as I mentored you into your new position here.' The lies continued as he rose and came towards me. '*Very* close . . .'

The abrupt pounding on the door knocked him offstride. He halted, throwing a confused look at the door and then at me. 'Are you expecting anyone?'

I shrugged. So far as I was concerned, it was the cavalry appearing on the horizon, the Marines storming over the hill with all bugles blowing – rescue! I dashed to open the door.

'Come in!' I welcomed. Nina was a bit of an anticlimax, but I was delighted to see her. Anyone would do.

'Come in!' I caught her arm and pulled her into the room.

'Oh –' Her face fell as she saw Ivor. 'It's you. Isn't anyone else here? I was looking for –'

'I haven't seen Petruchio all day,' I lied firmly. 'He certainly isn't here.'

'Petruchio? Who said anything about Petruchio?' She looked around wildly. 'I can't find Kiki!'

Chapter Twenty

Why was I not surprised?

'Kiki is having one of her migraine attacks,' Ivor said soothingly. 'She's been in bed with it for days. That's where you'll find her.'

'No! She isn't there!' Nina cried. 'She's not in her rooms. Her bed hasn't been slept in! I can't find her anywhere!'

'Then she must be feeling better and has gone out.' Ivor shrugged. 'Taking a bit of fresh air perhaps, after being cooped up in a darkened room feeling miserable.'

'You don't understand.' Nina looked so desperate that I felt sorry for her. Especially as I had a pretty good idea of what had happened to Kiki.

Young, female, blonde – and not seen in public for the past few days. Kiki fulfilled all the requirements to match the body I had discovered in the anchorite's cell. The body everyone had assured me had not existed. My own private hallucination.

Now Nina had discovered Kiki was missing – and was prepared to make a fuss about it. Would they try to persuade her that the absence of a body was *her* hallucination?

'We've got to find Kiki!' Nina looked wildly from me to Ivor. 'She isn't in the house – she must be somewhere in the grounds. Come and help me look!'

'Now?' Ivor shrank back. 'It's pitch black night out there. You'll never find her in the darkness. Wait until morning.'

'Morning could be too late! It's getting colder by the

minute – and it's raining again. She could die of hypo-thermia before morning.' Nina turned to me. 'Make him understand! Make him *do* something!'

A cold gust of wind hurled rain against the outer wall. The temperature seemed to plummet.

'Are you sure you've looked everywhere she might be?' I temporized. 'Even places where you wouldn't ordinarily expect to find her?' For the first time, I was in accord with Ivor, no more anxious to go outside than he was. Especially with what I knew – or suspected.

'Perhaps she's eloped.' Ivor offered an explanation Nina had accepted before. 'She wouldn't be the first one. Have you thought of that?'

'Who with?' Nina demanded scornfully. 'There haven't been any worthwhile visitors in months. That makes no sense!'

'But why should she be outside wandering around the grounds in this weather?' Ivor kept trying.

'Why not? Perhaps she's got amnesia.' Nina whirled and pointed an accusing finger at me. 'Nessa got it!'

She made it sound as though I were a role model. And an unsatisfactory one, at that.

'Amnesia wasn't anything I could help,' I protested. 'It was because of what happened to me – whatever that was.'

'Exactly!' Her triumphant tone said I had just proved her point. 'And who knows what's happened to Kiki? We've got to find her!'

'In the morning.' Ivor was unusually firm. 'It will be daylight then. And we can mobilize the guards to help search. If she hasn't come back by then.'

'You don't believe me!' She turned and appealed to me. 'You believe me, don't you?'

'I believe you can't find Kiki . . .' I said cautiously. 'But I'm not so sure she's wandering around somewhere out-side. The grounds are patrolled. Surely the guards would have found her before this. They found me.'

'That's true,' Ivor agreed. 'The guards are on constant alert to prevent trespassers –'

'Kiki isn't a trespasser – she *lives* here!'

They didn't notice that I went silent. If I mentally revised the tense Nina had used, I was not prepared to voice the correction. Looking at Ivor, I wondered if his reluctance to search for Kiki was due solely to the weather. Or did he, too, know that it would be a waste of effort?

'You're not going to help me – either of you!' The message had finally got through to Nina. 'All right, then, I'll find her myself!' She started for the door.

'Don't be a silly girl!' Ivor caught at her. 'You can't go running around in the rain and dark. You'll catch pneumonia. Or break an ankle. Or both . . .'

'Let go of me!' She twisted free and wrenched the door open. 'You can't stop me!'

Perhaps he couldn't, but there was an outbreak of sharp barks and growls outside. Nina shrieked and stumbled back into the room, followed by Bud and Brutus.

'Anything wrong here?' Bud asked.

Bud again. Had he taken up residence just beyond my door? If so, why? Did he feel especially protective towards Nessa because he had been the one to save her life? Perhaps the feeling had been there before that? Or was there a more sinister explanation: did he know what was going on around here?

'Nina's a bit overtired and upset,' Ivor told Bud, with a suggestive wriggle of his eyebrows that semaphored: *Tiresome hysterical female.*

'Oh, right,' Bud said. 'No real trouble then.'

'It *is* trouble!' Nina protested. 'The worst kind!' It was unfortunate that her voice was rising to a shriek, thereby reinforcing Ivor's message. 'Kiki is missing!'

'Is that so?' Bud was unmoved.

'It is!' Nina insisted. 'It is! We've got to find her! She could be lying in the moat – or a ditch somewhere – the way Nessa was.'

'There's no one in any moat, ditch, or under bushes on

this property.' Bud's eyes snapped; she was impugning his competence. 'We check all those places all the time. Especially after Miss Nessa –'

'I've told her that,' Ivor said. 'Perhaps she'll believe *you*.'

'Then where is she?'

The question hung there. I wasn't going to venture an opinion. This was Nina's show, let her get on with it. If she could.

The two men exchanged glances, while Nina glared at them accusingly, and reached the same conclusion: they were going to humour her. For the moment.

'There, there,' Ivor actually said, patting her shoulder. 'Everything will look better in the morning. You'll see . . .'

'We can do another check of the outbuildings when it's light,' Bud said. 'But we won't find anything.'

'Talk to Monica in the morning,' Ivor advised. 'Perhaps Kiki's migraine got worse and Monica packed her off to hospital with Dr Anderson.'

'No!' Nina wrenched away from Ivor's hand, which had patted its way down to her waist and was still heading south. 'I'd have known. She'd have sent a message.'

'Not necessarily. She may have been feeling too ill to think about that.' Ivor looked around for confirmation, but only Bud nodded.

I sank into a chair and closed my eyes to remind them that I was not a shining example of good health myself.

'We ought to let Miss Nessa get some rest.' Again, only Bud responded. 'She's not up to all this commotion right now.'

'Oh, yes . . . Yes, of course.' Ivor abandoned Nina and started towards me. 'You take Nina back to her quarters and I'll –'

'Actually –' I opened my eyes and met Bud's – 'they were *both* on the point of leaving.'

'That's what I thought.' The look Bud gave me made me wonder whether Anderson might not be my only candidate for brother-in-law. Quickly, I reappraised Bud: he was smarter than he first appeared. He seemed to be Chief

161

Guard. I had seen him giving instructions to the other guards and I would not be surprised to learn that he was really Oversall's Head of Security. There was more to him than met the casual eye.

'Right.' Meanwhile, he was ably herding my unwanted visitors towards the door, Brutus enthusiastically assisting him. 'See you in the morning,' he told me, closing the door behind them.

I took several deep breaths, enjoying the silence, then acknowledged that I still was not alone.

'You can come in now,' I told the waiting cat. 'They've gone.'

She strolled into the room, tail twitching, and gave me an accusing look.

'It wasn't my fault,' I said. 'I didn't invite them. It just happened.'

Not good enough. She prowled around the room, nose wrinkling at the disgusting smells. That dog again! In her territory! She was not happy.

Neither was I, but I had more to think about than an easily offended Dowager Duchess of a cat. Things were beginning to move.

Kiki's absence was finally attracting attention. If Nina made enough of a nuisance of herself about it, would they do something to explain it? Or would Anderson be called in again, with his useful little medicine kit and instant amnesia in his hypodermic?

It was getting late – but not that late. Perhaps this would be a good time to have a quiet word with Everett Oversall – now that I knew where he hid himself away. I was fairly certain I could find my way there again.

I threw on my shawl and went to the door. It wouldn't open. Another lock-in. For everyone – or just for me? And possibly Nina.

'So that's that!' I ripped off the shawl and hurled it at the sofa, addressing the cat. 'It looks like it's just you and me tonight.'

She stared at me enigmatically, then with a sort of

urgency. I had the feeling that there was some message she was trying to convey, but it was beyond my understanding.

'I'm sorry,' I said. 'I'm really sorry – but I just don't get it.'

She gave me a disgusted look, retreated to a far corner, sat down and began to wash her face.

Chapter Twenty-One

In the morning, Her Highness was still in an odd mood. She prowled restlessly, pausing every once in a while to glare at me. I was obviously deeply guilty of something.

But I had my own concerns. I wanted to get out of here before anyone could reach me to tell me I wasn't wanted in the PR office today either. Cautiously, I tried the outside door and was relieved when it opened smoothly. House arrest was over – for the time being.

The breakfast tray was sitting on the flagstones outside. I brought it in for a quick check: scrambled eggs and smoked salmon. Nice, but too easily tampered with. I'd give breakfast a miss this morning.

'Sorry,' I said, as the cat spoke sharply. 'I'm not going to test the stuff on you, no matter how much you volunteer.' She followed me, complaining loudly, as I went into the bathroom and flushed the food away.

That was the last straw for her. She stalked away, muttering imprecations. I had the feeling that 'Off with his head!' was the least of them. Oh, well, I'd try to make peace with her later.

Right now, I had to leave. The phone had begun to ring and I had no intention of answering it. The cat realized this and sat down glaring at me.

'Just don't answer it and it will stop ringing before long,' I told her, closing the door behind me and locking her in.

The answering yowl made me very glad that I couldn't translate it.

Ready to duck out of sight if I encountered anyone along the way, I reached the office block without any problems. Even as I walked along the corridor to my waiting desk, I saw no one but the town staff, who nodded pleasantly, but were unsurprised to see me. They had probably been told I wasn't well yesterday.

Candy's desk was unoccupied and there was no one else around from the senior staff.

The action was obviously taking place elsewhere – and I was pretty sure that Nina was in the middle of it. In fact, I would bet on it. Someone who was so single-minded in her pursuit of the peacocks and their feathers was not going to give up and go away quietly when her best friend had disappeared.

How far would Nina go with her concerns? And what would Everett Oversall do about them?

I settled down at my desk, pulled a stack of blank envelopes towards me and began work, keeping alert to any undercurrents that might be swirling below the surface.

It wasn't long before my fingers began to cramp, my throat felt so dry I could barely swallow and terminal boredom set in. I wondered how soon I could make some excuse to leave my desk. Or even if an excuse was necessary. No one appeared to be paying any attention to me.

Nor did they pay any attention to the telephone on Candy's desk when it rang several times before obviously being picked up on another line. Indifferent . . . or well-trained?

Probably the latter. If my experience was anything to go by, curiosity was discouraged around here. It was even quite probable that the day staff were deliberately brought in from outside so that no one knew too much about what went on here.

'There you are!' Candy appeared in the doorway, frowning at me. 'Where have you been? We've been looking for you!'

'Right here.' I widened my eyes. 'Where else would I be?'

'We never know. Never mind –' She gestured imperiously. 'Come along. You might be able to help.'

She led me to the real headquarters by a different route from the one I had discovered, but we were soon in a corridor I recognized – and I heard again the piano music coming from Yvonne's suite.

I could also hear the familiar shrieking when we were halfway down the hall. Nina in full flow. Not a sound for sore ears. The incoherent shrieks were punctuated by sobs and wails.

'It sounds as though Dr Anderson would be more help than me.'

'He's on the way,' Candy said tersely, not looking at me.

Was he, indeed? With his happy hypodermic? Perhaps two, one for Nina – and one for me, if I showed any signs of connecting the missing Kiki with the body I didn't quite remember finding in the anchorite's cell.

Keeping my face carefully blank, I followed Candy into what appeared to be Amanda's office. An enormous corkboard covered the wall behind a large desk. Invitations, newspaper clippings, press releases and an occasional postcard were pinned around the edges of the corkboard forming a thick border while the centre was given over to the pages of a month-at-a-glance calendar for last month, this month and next month, with various notations on most of the dates. A bookshelf contained copies of *Who's Who*, *Debrett's*, the *Almanach de Gotha* and other publications vital to the work of a social secretary.

'Nessa! You're here!' I flinched and stepped back as Nina hurled herself at me. I caught her arms before she could throw them around me and held her at a distance.

'Nessa!' she sobbed. 'Nessa! They don't believe me!' Implying that I did. We were off to a great start.

'Sit down.' It seemed the safest thing to say. 'Take it easy.' That wasn't bad, either. 'What's the matter?' I hoped would distance me a bit more.

'I told you!' She stepped back and looked at me incredulously. 'I told you last night!'

'You were so upset last night,' I murmured, with a craven shrug towards the others. 'Did you get any sleep at all?'

'Not much.' Answering the unexpected question, she was momentarily coherent, but it didn't last. 'How could I when –?'

'She's hysterical.' Yvonne was also keeping her distance, eyeing Nina with distaste. 'Again.'

'As usual,' Amanda agreed wearily. So that was the way they were going to play it.

'Dr Anderson will be here soon,' Candy said. 'He'll be able to give her something –'

'I don't want anything! I want to know where Kiki is!' Nina's voice began rising again. 'We've got to find her! She could be lying somewhere – hurt – unconscious –'

'Keep it down, will you!' Shadow appeared in the doorway, glaring at us, with an especially vicious look towards me. 'How do you expect Mr Oversall to concentrate on business when you're screaming the place down?'

'Tell him the situation is under control,' Yvonne said smoothly. 'There is nothing for him to concern himself with.'

'Oh, yes, there is!' Nina made a dash for the door, but Shadow blocked her way.

'Let me through! I've got to tell him! He'll help me! He *has* to!'

Eyebrows were raised and grimly amused looks exchanged. Everett Oversall didn't *have* to do anything.

'What's all this about?' Catching Nina by the shoulders, Shadow moved her across the room and into a chair with the expertise of a professional nurse – or bodyguard.

'She is unable to find Kiki,' Yvonne answered after a short pause. 'She believes Kiki has . . . gone missing.'

'And has she?'

'Who's keeping track?' Candy shrugged. 'We've all got better things to do.'

'The last any of us heard, Kiki had retired to bed with a migraine attack,' Amanda said. 'We haven't expected to see her for a while.'

'She's not in bed!' Nina wailed. 'She's not in her rooms!'

'Then perhaps she has moved somewhere else,' Yvonne said. 'Monica would know.'

Oh, yes, Monica would know. Monica, who had gone to investigate the cell after I had reported to her. Monica, who had cleared away the evidence and called Dr Anderson – not necessarily in that order. Monica would know – but would Monica tell?

Hah-bloody-hah!

'Monica *doesn't* know,' Nina said. 'I've already asked her.'

'Oh?' Again glances were exchanged over her head.

'Perhaps if one of *us* asked her . . .' Amanda suggested.

'Why should she tell you, if she wouldn't tell me?'

It was a fair question, from Nina's point of view, but no one seemed disposed to answer it.

'I want to see Mr Oversall!' Nina's mouth set stubbornly. 'I want to see him now!'

'It might not be a bad idea,' I said into the ensuing silence.

'Who asked you?' Shadow glared at me, then at the others as they hesitated. He didn't appear to like them any better.

'Get her out of here!' He threw out the order indiscriminately, jerking his thumb in Nina's direction, and this time I was included in the exchange of glances. 'I won't have Oversall disturbed!'

'Umm . . . why don't you take Nina back to your place?' Candy said to me. 'We'll have coffee sent over and you can . . .' She trailed off and I remembered she'd sought me out because she expected me to deal with Nina. *The glance stops here.*

'All right.' Why not? It wouldn't hurt to show willing

168

and, with Nina becoming increasingly agitated, I might even learn a bit more.

'Come on . . .' I slipped an arm around Nina's waist and urged her towards the door. 'Shhh . . . it's all right,' I soothed as she began to struggle. The door closed firmly behind us and it was safe to whisper. 'We'll go and check with Bud. He promised he'd search this morning, remember?'

'Oh . . . yes . . .' She relaxed and let me lead her outside. 'But no one said anything about a search.'

'I don't think Bud has to report to any of them. He seems to run his own operation – in his own way.'

'Yes . . .' She relaxed even more, perhaps with relief. 'Yes, you're right. Bud will –'

A flurry of urgent barks sent us hurrying across the lawn in their direction.

'Do you . . . think they've . . . found something?' Nina gasped.

'I don't know.' I couldn't tell her I doubted it, that I had reason to believe that all traces of anything to be found had been cleared away by now.

'Squirrels,' Bud said, patting Brutus to calm him. 'They're good dogs, but they're only human . . .' He paused and seemed to hear what he had just said.

'I mean,' he clarified, 'they've got these inbred instincts and sometimes they take over. The dogs can't help it.'

'Then . . .' Nina relinquished hope reluctantly. 'You haven't . . . found . . . anything?'

'Told you we wouldn't.' Bud was not without sympathy, but his expertise was in question. 'We run a tight ship here.'

But not tight enough to know anything the higher-ups might want to keep from him.

Or did he? Was he part of the conspiracy of silence? Was he helping to cover up whatever was going on? Security could mean a lot of things.

A low persistent buzzing began and Bud reached for a

holster on his belt that I had assumed held a gun and removed a cellphone instead.

'Security. Bud.' He spoke into it, then spent the remainder of the call listening.

'Right. I'll check on them,' he said, ending it and returning the phone to its holster. 'They're looking for you,' he told me. 'It seems coffee is being served in your quarters and you're not there.'

'That was quick,' I said. 'We just left the main house.'

'Things can move fast around here.' Was there an underlying meaning in his dry tone? 'I'll take you back, before anyone gets upset. They like to know where everybody is.'

'Except Kiki,' Nina said bitterly.

I might have known the unpleasant maid would be standing by my door with a heavy tray and a forbidding expression. No prizes for guessing who had reported that we hadn't immediately gone where we were sent like good little girls.

'Morning, Gerta.' Bud nodded before turning and leaving us safely delivered to what passed for home, his duty done.

'It's past noon!' she snapped after him. 'And I should be helping serve lunch in the canteen –' She transferred her complaints to us. 'Not wasting time waiting for someone to show up.'

'Where's Dilys?' I unlocked the door and she stormed past us to slam the tray down on a table. 'I thought she was taking care of me. I haven't seen her for ages.'

'Dilys has been reassigned.' The news didn't please me and she knew it. 'I'll be taking over her duties here.' That pleased me even less – and she gave me a grim knowing smile.

'Have *you* seen Kiki?' Nina asked abruptly.

'Not since her migraine started. We all have standing orders not to disturb the migraine sufferers when they're

170

having an attack.' Gerta gave a disbelieving sniff. 'There are a lot of them around here.'

So that was why no one had missed Kiki earlier. Not that I had the impression that anyone would have been concerned if they had.

A loud complaint at floor level caught our attention. The cat had appeared and was in full outraged Dowager Duchess mood. Tail lashing, she focused on me and berated me for some misdemeanour I had or had not committed.

'What's the matter with her?' Nina asked.

'Heaven knows,' I said. 'She's been in a strange mood for a long time. I don't know what her problem is.'

'You wouldn't!' Gerta sniffed, allowing her dislike and contempt to show. She stalked across the room and threw open the bathroom door. 'Can't you smell it?'

I exchanged a bewildered look with Nina and we both inhaled cautiously.

Now that Gerta mentioned it, there was a sharp faintly acrid odour emanating from the bathroom. No worse than I'd encountered in the dressing rooms of some of the gamier clubs I'd played, but –

'You were told –' Gerta eyed me sternly. 'They said if you wanted a cat, you had to look after it yourself. But –' again the disbelieving sniff – 'I suppose you don't remember that, either.'

'No. I don't.' I met the cat's accusing eyes and apologized. 'I'm sorry.'

'And so you should be!' Gerta spoke but, for a moment, I thought the cat had given voice. 'You can't expect *us* to do your nasty messy jobs. And the poor animal can't be expected to keep using a litter box in that condition. Cats have their self-respect, you know!'

A sharp yowl endorsed this sentiment. I should have known better. But how? I'd always moved around too much to take on any human baggage, let alone feline.

'I'm sorry,' I apologized again. 'I'll see to it just as soon as I can.'

I had to take care of Nina first. At least, I thought I did. I cast an anxious look at the cat, wondering how much longer she could keep her legs crossed.

A vaguely familiar buzzing began to make itself noticeable. Either I was developing tinnitus or – I was not altogether surprised when Gerta pulled a walkie-talkie from her apron pocket.

'Gerta here,' she said, then listened. 'Yes, yes. They are both here now. Yes, I will tell them, Mr Shadow.' She disconnected and returned the phone to her pocket.

'You are to remain here,' she instructed us with the officious note of delegated authority in her voice. 'You have enough food.' She indicated the tray filled with the ubiquitous sandwiches. 'If you require anything more, you can inform the kitchen –'

'Actually, I'm bored with all these sandwiches,' I said. 'We had enough of them yesterday. I'd rather have some fish and chips – double fish,' I added. It was the least I could do towards making peace with the Duchess. 'And a green salad and a decent bottle of chilled white wine.'

'I will give the kitchen your dinner order myself,' Gerta said pointedly. I needn't think I was going to get what I wanted immediately. For lunch, I could eat the sandwiches or go hungry – she didn't care which.

She gave me one final look of dumb insolence then, moving swiftly, as though fearing interception, she whisked herself through the door and was gone, not quite slamming it behind her.

'Well, well.' I stared after her, feeling that she had unintentionally given me a lot to think about. But right now I concentrated on the person who seemed to be my main adversary. 'So, it's *Mr* Shadow, is it? For a nurse – or even a bodyguard – he seems to take a lot on himself.'

'Nurse?' Nina looked at me blankly. 'Bodyguard? Oh, no. Or perhaps . . . a little. Just to look after his father. Along with the real work he does, learning everything.'

'His father?' It was my turn to look blank.

'He's Mr Overall's son.'

'His son? I never knew he had one.'

'He's kept it awfully quiet. I think he wants to give everyone one last shock when he dies and they find out. Kiki found out first, though, while she was doing the research for his autobiography. None of the others knew. She only told me – and maybe you.'

'If she did, I don't know it.' I shrugged. 'It's gone – along with almost everything else I ever knew.'

'Kiki said it was one of those business-arrangement marriages when Mr Oversall was just starting out. And it didn't last long enough for anyone to notice it. The poor woman died soon after having Shadow. But Mr Oversall did very well out of it: a son and a large chunk of a small Asiatic kingdom.'

'And he's kept it secret all these years?'

'With enough money, you can keep anything secret.' Nina frowned, as though she might be considering the implications of what she had just said. 'Oh, and there was another wife or two that Kiki discovered, but they'd died, too. Mr Oversall doesn't seem to have much luck with wives. Maybe that's why he gave up marrying.'

'Too many leftover in-laws.' It was another point for consideration. 'Making claims on him . . .'

'If they knew they were in-laws.' Nina's glance was surprisingly shrewd. 'Maybe he had more reason than one to keep everything so quiet.'

'And there was never a whisper of any of this in the media,' I marvelled.

'No, and there probably won't be – until he dies.' The mere thought made Nina highly uncomfortable and she rushed into denial. 'But that won't be for years and years yet.'

Oh, won't it? Had Nessa discovered something to the contrary? And was that why someone had tried to dispose of her? And why Shadow hated her so much?

And could the same hold true for Kiki, who had been delving into old records? What else might she have discovered that the reclusive Everett Oversall wanted to keep secret?

A sharp remark from the still-offended Dowager Duchess reminded me that there were more immediate practical considerations to attend to.

'Sorry,' I said. 'I think I'd better –'

'That's all right,' Nina said. 'I wasn't planning to stay, anyway. Only long enough to make sure Gerta was out of the way before I left.'

She crossed to the door and opened it carefully, peeking out and shuddering. 'It's getting dark again. More rain. I've got to find Kiki. I have the most awful feeling –'

She was right. But I couldn't tell her so.

'Be careful,' I said. 'Be very careful.'

'Yes.' She looked at me and, for the first time, all the artiness and pretentiousness dropped away from her. 'Yes, I know.'

Chapter Twenty-Two

'All right,' I said to the Duchess as the door closed behind Nina. 'Now let's see about you.'

She followed me into the bathroom and led me over to the elaborate mock-cottage that housed her litter box. I'd noticed it there in the corner, but hadn't actually connected it with any practical use. Some decoration of Nessa's, I'd assumed, perhaps something left over from her scenery designing days.

The chimney acted as the handle. A cautious pull and the whole edifice lifted off, revealing the unpleasant mess it had been designed to conceal. The cat and I both retreated a couple of paces from the revolting smell now fully released into the room. She gave me an accusing look.

'How was I to know?' I tried to defend myself. 'I thought the cleaners took care of things like this.' Actually, I hadn't thought about it at all and the look she gave me told me she knew it.

'Right.' I avoided her gaze. 'Let's sort this out now.' With the house removed, I found a sack of kitty litter and several folded bin bags had been hidden in the corner behind it, along with a supply of small plastic sheets which were obviously used to line the litter box itself.

I shook out a bin bag and, holding my breath, bundled liner, used litter and all into it. As I replaced the litter tray on the floor, I noticed that something that had been beneath the liner was still in it.

I gave the tray another shake, but couldn't dislodge the

thing. At least it had been under the liner, I consoled myself, reaching for it.

It didn't come away without a struggle and I saw that it had been roughly glued to the tray.

The cat gave an impatient yowl and I tossed the thing to one side as I relined and refilled the tray. First things first. The cat stepped into the tray, pawed at the litter, smoothing it out, then looked up at me huffily.

'Oops, sorry.' I got the message and covered both cat and tray with the concealing house. A lady had a right to her privacy.

I retrieved the object I had discovered in the litter tray and gave it my full attention. It seemed to be a little square plastic envelope – the sort collectors use for small objects of value: stamps, coins, medals, that sort of thing.

Had Nessa decided to become a collector? Of what? I turned the envelope over, looking for the opening. Whatever it was, it was concealed by a folded paper wrapped around it, perhaps for extra protection.

For what? A Penny Black stamp? No – there was something round and hard inside that paper. A rare coin? Perhaps a valuable medal from some historic battle?

Something worth having – and hiding. Small, valuable – and extremely portable. The sort of thing war refugees – and fugitives – invested their funds in when they knew they might have to flee a country suddenly.

Nessa – prepared to run away?

The opening was beneath the dollop of glue I scraped aside. The enclosing wrapper made it a tight fit inside the tiny container. I eased it out and tried not to tear the paper while I released its contents.

I had no doubt that this was what everyone had been searching for. But surely no one around here was so short of money that they had to resort to thievery. Unless it was valuable beyond the dreams of avarice?

Yet I had the uneasy feeling that they had not known really what they were looking for – just hoping to recognize it when they saw it.

Except, perhaps, for Ivor. He had tried to open the smallest drawer in the desk. *What did he know?*

I worked away at the tightly folded paper, my disquiet stirring as my fingertips told me there was something odder here than I had imagined.

Of course, there were ancient Chinese coins with a hole in the centre. Probably any number of ancient civilizations had once minted gold currency neatly hollowed so that it could be strung on a rope or chain for easy carrying . . .

The object burst free suddenly and fell to the floor. I stared down at it, unwilling to believe the information my eyes were relaying to my brain.

It was a ring. A plain gold ring. A wedding ring.

I stooped and retrieved it, vaguely aware that I was shaking my head in a denial I knew was useless.

Nessa? Nessa? Married? And never told me?

Worse – I'd had no inkling of it. How had there been such a failure of that sixth sense that had always operated between us?

Unless –? I grasped wildly at the faint hope – explanation – that occurred to me: perhaps the ring wasn't hers. She had found it somewhere and it . . . it . . .

I carried the ring over to the brightest table lamp and squinted at the smooth flat inside surface. There were initials engraved on it. My eyes blurred suddenly and I couldn't read them.

I didn't want to read them. Before the blurring, I had seen the *V* for *Vanessa.* Were the corresponding initials *B.A.* for *Brian Anderson*? Or even *Bud*? What the hell kind of name was Bud, anyway? Not a name, a nickname, that's all. If I saw his real initials, I wouldn't recognize them.

Just as long as there wasn't an *I* for *Ivor! No. Nessa, you couldn't have!* There was no way he –

The blurring cleared and I had to force myself to look at the inscription again. The letters danced, blurred, then settled into focus:

E.L.O.

Who? The *L* threw me momentarily. Unwanted knowledge thumped at my consciousness, but I refused to acknowledge it. I didn't want to believe it. I wouldn't believe it! I looked around wildly.

The paper that had been folded so tightly around the ring lay on the table beside the lamp where I had dropped it. There was printing on one side of the paper – and handwriting. I picked it up slowly and smoothed it out.

A marriage certificate.

Vanessa Elfrida Miller . . . and . . . Edward Llywellyn . . . Overall . . .

Shadow? Shadow was my brother-in-law? But . . . he hated Nessa. It was in every look he gave me, every fibre of his being when he had to be near me.

I looked at the date on the certificate . . . barely six months ago. It hadn't taken long for the bloom to go off *that* rose.

Nessa – what happened? In so short a time?

And then I looked at the other dates. Looked . . . and again couldn't believe what I was seeing.

It wasn't Shadow Nessa had married – it was the old man himself.

All the while I had been mentally auditioning prospective candidates, the position was already filled.

Everett Overall, billionaire. My brother-in-law.

And *that* was why Shadow hated Nessa. I saw again the fury in his eyes, heard the hatred and contempt in his voice as he flung the word at me like an obscenity: *Mother!*

A stepmother who was young enough to have been his own bride. Was that part of his problem? Or was the mere fact of it more than his pride could bear?

And had he done any more about it than seethe and brood? Had he been the one who had tried to murder Nessa? Who was now prowling the cloister in the monk's robe, trying to entice me outside so that he could try again?

Mr Overall doesn't seem to have much luck with wives. Nina's words came back to me. She thought he'd stopped trying. It appeared that he had gone for one last throw of the dice – and his luck was still rotten.

But not as bad as Nessa's. What had she walked into, in this nest of serpents?

A sudden pressure on my ankles startled me and I jumped, then looked down to find the Duchess twining around them. We were back on friendly terms again; in fact, we were getting positively intimate.

'Feeling better?' Chancing my luck, I stooped and picked her up. Far from protesting, she settled into my arms and began purring. I felt myself grow calmer as I stroked her. Some of the disquieting images faded from my mind and I was able to think more clearly.

I had to talk to Everett Oversall; he held the key to all this.

Key. That inspired another thought. Still holding the cat, I went to the door and tried to open it. As I had suspected, it refused to yield.

My own private lock-in. Again.

Was Nina locked in, too? If she had gone back to her studio, that is. If she wasn't wandering around the grounds, still caught up in her hopeless search for Kiki.

As though she understood that I had just been thwarted in an attempt to leave her, the cat's purring increased and she twisted her head to get an extra-good rubbing behind first one ear and then the other. We were going to have a nice intimate evening all on our own.

'That's right,' I said. 'It's just you and me tonight.' And possibly just as well. It would give me time to digest what I had learned and decide just how I was going to deal with my newly discovered brother-in-law. Or husband, if I stayed in character.

Only . . . there was still something nagging at the back of my mind. I stood silent and motionless, waiting to see if it would come to me.

After a long moment, it did – and I received a sharp complaint as my fingers tightened abruptly around a furry neck.

Anderson!

Kiki was missing . . . Nina was hysterical. Dr Anderson had been sent for and was expected to arrive promptly to attend to her.

But he had never shown up.

Where the hell was he? Had he gone missing, too? What had happened to him? Had he been delayed, or –?

Chapter Twenty-Three

I woke in the morning with such an overwhelming feeling of well-being that it unnerved me. There was no reason for it. Things weren't going *that* well.

They were progressing. I had found the ring and the marriage certificate. But now I had to decide what to do with them. Nothing to be so cheerful about there.

But I could feel my lips curving in a smile, there was a warmth in the region of my heart. Also . . . a certain heaviness.

I opened my eyes to find the cat curled on my chest. A receding memory told me that she had been there all night. She had accepted me at last.

She stirred, as though aware of being watched, opened her eyes to look into mine – and began purring.

There were worse ways to start the day. But, pleasant as this was, it still didn't fully account for my ridiculously good mood.

Unless – I closed my eyes and waited . . . listened . . . questioned . . . holding my breath, scarcely daring to hope.

Somewhere deep inside of me there came a faint answering flicker, a tendril of another consciousness reaching out to me, trying to contact me . . .

Nessa was back! Conscious. Compos mentis. And calling to me.

I concentrated all my energy, trying to answer her, to beam encouragement and strength to her.

I felt a momentary response, then it faded, perhaps

as she drifted off into what I sensed would now be a healing sleep.

Now, more than ever, I needed to talk to Dr Brian Anderson. He was supposed to keep me informed. Perhaps I had discouraged that when I jumped all over him for detaching Nessa from her life support system without consulting me, her next of kin.

Except that – in the strictly legal sense – I was no longer her next of kin. Everett Oversall was – a spouse took precedence. Had Anderson known about the marriage?

Madame knew. I had studied the marriage certificate until I had memorized it last night. I could understand and agree with Oversall that Everett was a more impressive name for professional use than Edward. In the theatre world, people who changed their names were more usual than those who didn't.

The names of the witnesses were more interesting. At least, the one I was able to identify as Madame's was. The other was male, Middle Eastern and unknown to me – probably some passing-through business associate of Oversall's who had been co-opted to stand witness at the registrar's office, sign the certificate, and be sent on his way without ever having full comprehension of the importance of the event he had witnessed. He might not even have spoken or understood English.

Madame, however, was a different story.

I finished dressing, a thorough job, with jeans and pullover beneath the kaftan, so that I could revert to my own form if I got the chance to slip away from this place and make it to the hospital to check on Nessa.

The cat watched disapprovingly as I refolded the marriage certificate into a less bulky size and slid it between the pages of one of the books, which I then replaced on the shelf.

Next I raided Nessa's jewel box for a thin gold chain, threaded it through the wedding ring and fastened the chain around my neck, concealing the ring in my bodice in the time-honoured tradition.

As a final touch, I added eyeliner, mascara, blusher and several more gold chains, to be worn outside this time. Dress to kill – or be killed.

Now for Madame.

Bud intercepted me just before I reached Madame's cottage. I wondered if he had followed me from the cloister.

'You're looking better every day,' he greeted me. Had I put on too much make-up? Brutus, too, was regarding me with unusual interest.

'I'm feeling better,' I said, moving downwind of the dog's twitching nose.

'Taking a little stroll before you start the day's work, are you?'

Keeping tabs on me, are you?

'That's right.' I smiled demurely. 'I thought I'd drop in on Madame and see how she is this morning.' He could guess that for himself, no harm in confirming it. 'That is, if Richie will let me see her. I don't think he likes me. Or else he's afraid I'll tire Madame. I won't, I promise.'

'I believe you.' He regarded me speculatively. 'Would you like me to get him out of the way for you?'

'Would you?' The way he was looking at me made me wary about promising any sort of gratitude. I turned it into a challenge, instead. 'Can you?'

'Just watch me.' He marched down the path, Brutus trotting at his heel.

I moved out of sight and waited.

When Bud emerged, Richie was with him. They moved off in the direction of the woods with some urgency. Behind Richie's back, Bud signalled a thumbs-up to me.

The coast was clear.

'Ah, Vanessa.' In the front room, Madame was waiting. 'I have been expecting you.' *Will you walk into my parlour?* 'I knew you would return.'

'Did you?' I took the chair she indicated. 'I think you know more about me than I do.'

'Would that be so hard?' Those hooded eyes watched me expectantly. 'Unless you have begun to remember?'

When you remember, I'll be waiting . . . Had that message come from Madame?

'Not really. Oh, there are moments when something seems familiar, but I don't know whether it's a memory trying to surface, or because I've been back long enough to start to get into a routine. I've been hoping you could tell me . . . help me . . . but it isn't easy to get in to see you.'

'Ah, yes. But Richie is not here now. Bud has just called him away on some problem. I had wondered when he claimed that it was so urgent.' She gave me a sharp look. 'You were always a favourite with Bud. With most of the men.'

'But not the women?'

'*Pah!*' she spat. 'They do not like anyone, not even each other. Least of all, each other!'

'Jealousy?'

'The place reeks of it! Writhes with it! Have you not noticed? I thought you had only lost your memory – not your wits!'

'I appreciate the vote of confidence, but we haven't much time. Let's get down to business.'

'Vanessa –?' She looked at me uncertainly. I had spoken too sharply, too forcefully. 'Vanessa, you seem . . . different.'

'One can't stay an ingénue for ever – and murder attempts *do* tend to concentrate the mind. Or even what's left of it.'

'You believe someone tried to kill you?' She nodded slowly. 'I would not say you were wrong. But, if you remember nothing, what can be done?'

'And not just me,' I said. 'What about Kiki?'

'Kiki?' She shrugged. 'These girls – they come and they

go. They arrive believing that fortune has favoured them – that Everett is in their thrall, that it is only a matter of time before he gives them everything they want.' She watched intently for my reaction.

I did not think you were so greedy, she had said once. Knowing what I now knew, I suspected that that must mean Nessa had signed a pre-nuptial agreement before the wedding. Just the sort of thing Nessa would do – throw away her chance of a fortune if – when – the marriage hit the rocks. I couldn't believe it would last. Obviously, neither could Oversall.

'And slowly they understand that they are just another distraction . . .' Madame continued, disappointed by my lack of reaction. 'An amusement . . . a toy. So they get angry, very angry, and rush back to their former lives.'

'I don't think Kiki left in a huff,' I said. 'I think she left in a coffin.'

'You have reason to think this?' I'd seen ventriloquists move more facial muscles than Madame did as she asked. 'Apart from your own experience?'

'All I know about my own experience is hearsay,' I reminded her. 'And so is everything I've heard about Francesca . . .?'

'Kiki . . .? Francesca . . .?' Madame sighed. 'So many questions. Always questions, Vanessa. Why could you never leave well enough alone?'

'Well enough?' I was suddenly furious. 'Well enough for whom? Certainly not for them! Nor for me – if someone had had their way.'

'So now you ask.' Madame nodded sadly. 'For Francesca, for Kiki, for yourself. So many questions. And who is there to answer?'

'I was hoping you would.'

'Why should I know these things?'

'I think you know a great many things. And I think it's time you told them.'

'Time? We are all prisoners of time . . . and with only one way to escape our captor.'

'Madame!' I tried to control my irritation, but lost. 'Stop stalling!' It was too abrupt again, too emphatic, but she didn't seem to notice, or perhaps she was just getting used to it.

'Madame,' I said more gently. 'I may not have recovered my memory, but I have found something else.' I had her full attention as I separated the thin gold chain from the others and tugged on it, slowly bringing the gold band into view.

She leaned back in her chair and closed her eyes, exhaling a long regretful sigh.

'I believe this gives me the right to some answers,' I said. 'The wedding certificate was with it – and it carried your name as one of the witnesses. What –?'

'It is for Everett to say!' She interrupted me imperiously. 'Take me to him!'

'Right!' I swung her wheelchair around, through the narrow doorway, down the hall and out on to the path.

'To the right,' she directed. 'There is a short cut.'

It was a nasty shock to round the corner at the end of the hedge and encounter Ivor. I resisted temptation and stopped short. I wouldn't have minded running him down, although there was a limit to the amount of damage a wheelchair could do, but Madame was a precious cargo and I didn't want to risk harming her.

'Vanessa!' He recoiled as though he had sensed my thought. Or as though he had seen a ghost. 'What are you doing with Madame?'

'I am taking the air,' Madame informed him icily.

'Where's her lap rug?' He frowned at me accusingly. 'She'll catch her death of cold. Take her home immediately!'

'I will go where I choose, when I choose!' It seemed that Madame found him as insufferable as I did. 'If you continue to block my way, *you* will be responsible for any illness I may contract – and be assured that Everett will know it!'

'I . . . I didn't mean . . .' Ivor backed down immediately and moved away. 'I . . . I'll just . . .' He fled.

'Hurry!' Madame snapped. 'He will tell! He always tells! He will send Richie to stop me. Push faster!'

Chapter Twenty-Four

Monica opened the door after I had inadvertently knocked by bumping the footplate of the wheelchair into it.

'Madame –' She smiled, then looked up at me and the smile faded. 'Vanessa –'

'Bring them in!' Everett Oversall's voice overrode hers.

'Yes, of course.' She stepped back and allowed me to wheel Madame past her.

Oversall was seated behind his desk. His eyes flickered as he took a good look at me – and then focused at a point high on my chest.

I realized I had not replaced the ring beneath the neckline of my kaftan.

Had Ivor noticed? Was that what had sent him into retreat and not Madame's annoyance?

'Over there,' Madame commanded. 'Beside the desk.'

I placed her as directed, swinging the chair around so that she faced outwards into the room. It was then that I saw him.

Dr Brian Anderson. Standing off to one side, trying to be unobtrusive, looking as though he wished he were somewhere else. Anywhere else. Looking guilty.

I met his eyes and he flushed.

'Vanessa wishes to speak to you.' Madame addressed Everett Oversall, but she looked pointedly at Monica as she added, 'In private.'

'Of course.' Monica inclined her head graciously, but the question in her eyes was apparent. No one answered it.

'Oh!' She nearly collided with Anderson as he dived for the door.

'Not you!' Oversall's voice halted him. 'You stay!'

'Um, er . . .' Anderson ducked his head and gave an awkward grimace, obviously wishing he could produce a good excuse for getting out of there. He looked at Oversall, he looked at Madame. He looked everywhere – except at me.

We all held our places in a silent tableau until the door had closed behind Monica. We waited until we heard her footsteps fading away down the corridor. Then the atmosphere changed. Not relaxed, just changed.

'So, Vanessa,' Oversall said. 'Any improvement in your memory . . . my darling?'

Anderson winced. Madame twisted her head to look at Oversall strangely.

The door opened again and both Shadow and Richie advanced into the room, glaring at me.

'I did not ring!' Oversall stopped them with an imperious gesture.

'You are not required!' Madame's gesture mirrored his. 'Leave!'

Neither of them moved. Richie kept his eyes on Madame, his body tensed, as though he might dash forward, seize the wheelchair and sweep her away.

Shadow concentrated on me, his burning gaze the sort that made me profoundly grateful that looks couldn't kill; if they could, I would be a heap of smouldering ashes.

Instinctively, I looked to Everett Oversall for . . . what? Reassurance? Protection? Whatever he had to offer his presumed wife when his son was channelling hatred and malice towards her.

'Quite right, Vanessa,' he said. 'We need more discipline around here. Shadow –' His voice whiplashed through the room. 'Either treat your mother with the proper respect or . . .' His voice fell away in some implied threat that must be too familiar to both of them to need repeating.

Shadow was in trouble – and it was my fault. Those

blazing eyes left me in no doubt of that. Nor that he would get me for it. Somewhere . . . sometime . . .

'Shadow!' The velvet glove was off – if it had ever been on.

'Richie!' He was going to brook no insubordination from the hired help, either.

They came to heel. Slowly and reluctantly. Madame nodded with satisfaction at their lowered heads, their submissive postures.

'Shadow –' Overall directed. 'Go and tell Monica that I will be joining them at dinner this evening. You,' he added pointedly, 'will not. Nor will Richie. I will speak to you both here in the morning.'

That was it. The silence lengthened and seemed to thicken until, slowly, Shadow and Richie turned and left the room.

'Now then, Vanessa.' Overall turned to me.

'Now then . . . my love,' I riposted, one hand reaching for the wedding ring and clinging to it ostentatiously.

Anderson flinched and looked desperately from Overall to me and back again. Madame just sat there, only her eyes moving, not missing a trick.

I wished I did have a trick or two up my sleeve.

'Please sit down, Vanessa.' There was a note in Overall's voice that disturbed me. 'After all, you're still convalescent. You must take care of yourself.'

No one else will – was that the message he meant to convey?

'I intend to.' I sank into the armchair he indicated. 'Thank you.'

'You're more than welcome.' He watched me steadily. 'My love.'

I smiled at him with a blandness I didn't feel. If he was trying to make me nervous, he was succeeding. But damned if I would show it!

'Everett –?' Madame looked at him uncertainly. 'Vanessa –?' She transferred her gaze to me.

Neither of us responded.

190

Anderson edged a little closer to the door.

'Vanessa wished to speak to you, Everett,' Madame said. 'That is why we are here.'

'Only speak? How disappointing. I'd hoped she might be ready to take her rightful place . . . by my side. Or is that what we're going to speak about . . . my darling?'

I stared at him. The more he talked, the less I liked his tone. Or what he was implying.

'What's the matter? Cat got your tongue . . . Vanessa?'

Suddenly, he convulsed, bending low until his forehead nearly struck the top of his desk.

'Everett!' Madame cried in alarm. She, too, thought he was having some sort of fit.

I stood and started forward. Anderson, however, despite the wheezing choking noises coming from his employer, did not move to help. In fact, he backed a little farther towards the door.

Oversall straightened up and I discovered he was laughing. He was amused . . . toying with me –

He knew!

'You bastard!' Anderson couldn't move fast enough to escape me. I caught him by the shirt front, raised him up on his toes and slammed him against that door he'd been so anxious to reach. 'You told!'

'Vanessa!' I heard Madame gasp behind us. Oversall was still laughing.

'Don't be a fool, man!' Anderson clawed at my hands, trying to free himself. 'He had to know. Did you really think I could keep a desperately ill patient in the intensive care unit without anyone knowing? Without accounting to anyone? Without authorization?'

'He authorized you to take her off the life support machine!' That still rankled. 'Without consulting me.'

'I was right.' Oversall had stopped laughing. 'She was responding and didn't need it any more. She's growing stronger every hour now.'

'She's still far from well,' Anderson warned. 'It will take more time – but she's going to make it.'

'I want to see her.' I lowered Anderson to his feet, but kept hold of his shirt. 'Take me to town! Now!'

'It won't do any good,' he said. 'She isn't there.'

'Where is she?' I began to hoist him again.

'In a safe haven,' Oversall cut in. 'We moved her when Kiki . . . disappeared. We didn't want anything to happen to her. Not anything more.'

Something hit the back of my ankles and I lost my grip on Anderson. He scuttled away. I turned to look down at Madame – she had rammed me with the footplate of her wheelchair.

'That wasn't kind,' I said.

'Neither is your behaviour . . . Vanessa. Only you are not Vanessa. Almost – but not quite. Who are you?'

'Her twin.' I did Madame the courtesy of retaining my natural voice. 'Her fraternal twin – Vance. I apologize for the deception, but it was necessary.' I offered her my hand.

'I see.' After a long moment, she accepted my hand in a surprisingly strong grip. I had the feeling that she did see – or almost.

'Everett –' She swung about to face him. 'Why did you not tell me?'

'The fewer who knew, the better.' Oversall looked faintly uncomfortable.

'Oh?' She shot him an *I'll speak to you later* look. 'And Kiki has disappeared?'

'Kiki is dead,' I said, since it seemed no one else was going to. 'I found her body. And *then* someone disappeared it.'

'So? Everett?' She looked to him for an explanation.

He shook his head. She wasn't going to get one. Not here. Not now.

'Everett –' Maybe she wasn't, but I was. 'Or should I say Edward, brother Edward?' For a moment, I was distracted by a sudden vision of him in a monk's robes, stalking the cloister.

No! I shook off the image, intriguing though it was.

Overall didn't operate that way – he didn't need to do his own dirty work. Apart from that, why should he? Even if Nessa had learned something deeply incriminating about him, he had already neutralized any possible threat from her. A wife could not be forced to testify against her husband.

'What's your game?' I demanded. 'Where did Nessa fit into it? Why would anyone want to kill her? What was she doing here in the first place? Why did you –?'

'Wait!' Overall held up a hand to stop me. 'If you're not going to stop for breath, I can't get a word in edgewise, far less answer any questions.'

'Go ahead then.' I clenched my teeth. 'Talk!'

'We have been having a bit of trouble here for some time . . .' Overall paused and exchanged a grim look with Madame.

'An enemy within,' she supplied.

'A spy,' he corrected. 'An industrial spy. Highly confidential information has been finding its way into the hands of competitors who have used it against me. The information had to be coming from this headquarters, which meant I could not trust anyone already in residence. I imported Francesca from an Italian subsidiary to look into the matter. She was clever, ambitious, multilingual but, just when she seemed to be getting to grips with the problem . . .' He shrugged. 'She disappeared – or so they tell me.'

'You don't believe them?'

'I seldom believe everything I am told. Francesca left without giving notice or telling anyone, she took few belongings with her, the salary paid into her account was never touched. In fact, there has been no financial activity – either with bank account or credit cards – since she "eloped". That is all I know.'

'But not all you suspect?'

'How could it be?' He lowered his head for a moment. 'Then, more than ever, I needed to know more.'

'And that's where Nessa came in?'

'After Francesca, it seemed . . . wiser . . . to bring in a complete outsider, someone who had nothing to do with –' his lips twisted – 'the "Oversall Empire", as the tabloids like to call it. I've begun dabbling in the entertainment world recently, strictly for my own amusement, and I met Vanessa when I invested in a show she was designing. She was restless, not happy – a love affair gone wrong, I gathered. She was no longer sure she wished to continue working in the theatre. She was looking around for something else that would be interesting . . . present a challenge. She was open to an offer.'

'So she married you?' I couldn't keep the incredulity out of my voice. He was not exactly Love's Young Dream – even on the rebound – unless we were talking about Gold Diggers. And Vanessa wasn't greedy.

'Not immediately. That wasn't part of the original plan. She was just to take over where Francesca had left off and see what she could discover.'

'But?' There was always a but.

'But . . .' He nodded acknowledgement. 'Circumstances change . . . new issues emerge –'

'There was a fresh betrayal,' Madame interrupted. 'A most serious betrayal. It was necessary for Everett to take steps to protect his interests – and himself.'

'And he did that by marrying Nessa? Wouldn't it have been simpler just to call in the police?'

'Then the situation couldn't be kept under wraps. There are always leaks when too many are involved. Inevitably, the media would learn that Oversall Enterprises had been defrauded of millions. We'd lose the confidence of our associates – and quite rightly. Our integrity would be compromised, we would –'

'We would look like fools!' Madame snapped. 'We would become a laughing stock. It was necessary to take steps to avoid this.'

'And Vanessa was one of those steps?' I found myself shaking with fury.

'Vanessa understood the situation,' Oversall said mildly. 'She was in complete agreement with us.'

'So much so that she agreed to marry you? Agreed to sign the pre-nuptial agreement –'

'There was no pre-nuptial agreement,' Oversall said. 'That was the whole point of the exercise. The marriage nullified my current will and many of the long-standing staff arrangements. If anything happened to me, Vanessa would inherit everything.'

'It was a form of insurance to see that nothing would happen to Everett.' Madame nodded her head emphatically.

'No – it happened to Vanessa instead! You deliberately threw her into the firing line to preserve your rotten hides!'

'Not quite. Vanessa was my secret weapon. Only my most-trusted Madame knew of the marriage. Vanessa would continue in her usual way. No one would know anything had changed. If anyone learned of our secret – then we had found our traitor.'

'Except that it didn't quite work that way.'

'Nothing happened for months. Vanessa returned to her quarters and life went on as normal, except that we were now on guard. Waiting . . . Another betrayal and I would announce our marriage, emphasizing that Vanessa was now my sole heir and making sure all the implications of that were clear.'

Interesting. Did he understand that he had as good as admitted that he didn't trust Shadow – his own son – any more than I did?

'Meanwhile,' he went on, 'Security kept a close eye on Vanessa during the day, but perhaps not so close at night . . .'

'They do now.' I thought of my frequent encounters with Bud and Brutus.

'Once she had bolted herself in for the night, we thought she was safe. She was aware that the situation was tricky, she knew better than to admit any callers – or allow herself to be lured outside – after dark . . .

'And yet . . . she went outside that night . . .' He shook his head. 'I can't imagine what possessed her to be so careless.'

'Perhaps that was the first time the Monk began prowling – she didn't know what was happening and was curious.' That was the best explanation I could think of. But, even so, I wouldn't have thought Nessa would be so curious – or so impulsive – as to chase him. So careless . . .

'What is done is done,' Madame pronounced. 'And only we know the real result of it.'

I found I didn't like the speculative way Madame was regarding me.

'Quite.' Oversall, too, had a look in his eyes that chilled me. 'But now we have our Vanessa back again – and even more of a threat to person or persons unknown should her memory return . . .'

'You mean,' I said, 'you're going to use me as bait.'

'Use you?' Oversall gave me a vulpine smile. 'I was under the distinct impression that you'd long since volunteered.'

Chapter Twenty-Five

We had our aperitifs in Oversall's apartment before making a delayed Grand Entrance in the dining room. Anderson wheeled Madame's chair; I walked at Oversall's side, my arm in his.

It was all there: the heads snapping up, the indrawn breaths, the eyes that followed our every move. Ah, yes, the stars had entered and the stage was ours. All that was missing was the applause.

I wasn't wearing the wedding ring; it didn't fit. So it still swung proudly and blatantly from the chain around my neck. Let them all wonder about it. I didn't catch anyone actually staring at it, but I was sure no one had missed it.

Shadow wasn't there – but the hatred was. I glanced at Oversall, at Madame. Could they feel it, too?

I saw that Anderson was no stranger to the usual arrangements as he slotted Madame neatly into her place beside mine and took Richie's accustomed chair on her other side. He did not look at all happy about it.

'My dear . . .' Oversall bowed me into my chair and took the place usually occupied by Monica – on my left at the head of the table.

Monica was opposite him at the foot of the table, her smile rather strained.

The others were all present and accounted for, in their usual places. Only Nina looked pleased to see me.

Ivor, after one swift glance, ignored me. Candy inspected me more closely, taking in my mascara, blusher and more emphatic lipstick, then gave me an approving nod. I was beginning to make more of myself, as she had suggested.

Amanda and Yvonne barely acknowledged our arrival, their body language conveying that they were absorbed in some vital conversation of their own, which was much too important for them to take any notice of extraneous details – like the unusual presence of Overall at the table. Or the unusual attention he was paying to me.

'I haven't seen you all day.' Nina was paying attention, too. 'I was beginning to get worried.'

'I've been . . . resting,' I said.

'It's done you good,' she said. 'You look a lot better. Oh! Not that you didn't look all right before.'

'She is stronger,' Madame said. 'She grows stronger every day. It is good.'

'And more beautiful, too.' Overall laid it on with a trowel.

'Why, thank you . . .' I fluttered my eyelashes at him . . . 'Everett.'

A tidal wave of hatred struck me. Yet no face changed. I wondered if Shadow were lurking nearby. Eavesdropping . . . afraid of missing something . . . feeding his hatred.

The service door opened and the first course arrived. Gerta shot me a nasty look as she set a bowl of leek-and-potato soup down in front of me. She might not actually hate me, but she certainly disliked me. To be fair, she didn't seem to like any of the others, either.

The soup was delicious. Perhaps the knowledge that someone was begrudging me every spoonful made me savour it more.

'It's so very good to have you back among us once more, my dear,' Overall said fulsomely. 'I know I speak for all of us.'

Wicked man! My sardonic look to him must have passed as a flirtatious one. A ripple of suppressed fury surged through the atmosphere like lightning before a storm broke.

'True, true!' Ivor lurched to his feet, wine glass raised. 'A toast! Vanessa – your health! Your continued very good health!'

Chairs were pushed back awkwardly as everyone except Madame stood and raised their glasses.

'Good health,' they echoed, although I would be prepared to bet that not many of them actually drank. They were all looking at Oversall and not at me.

'Thank you, Everett, Ivor – all of you.' It was my turn. I stood and raised my own glass. 'To all of you – who have been so generous in sharing your memories with me, in an attempt to help me regain mine.' I took a hearty gulp and sat down.

Wicked man! Oversall's sardonic look mirrored my own and threw it back at me. The old devil was enjoying this.

'Well said, my dear.' He moved swiftly to refill my glass personally, a mark of favour no one missed.

There was a sharp sniff by my ear as Gerta snatched away my soup bowl and went on to collect the rest of them. Monica must have quietly signalled the end of the course.

The soup was immediately replaced by crown roast of lamb with roast potatoes, buttered leeks and green beans with toasted flaked almonds.

'Aaah . . .' Oversall looked at his plate with deep satisfaction before lifting his knife and fork. 'My compliments to the chef.'

Someone poured a rich red wine into the appropriate glasses while we all followed his lead and there was a peaceful silence as everyone concentrated on the meal.

Oversall saw fit to enliven the proceedings by occasionally patting my hand and giving me a fond smile. I forced myself not to pull my hand away. I may have agreed to act as bait, but did he have to cut me up quite so much?

By the time the gooseberry syllabub was served, barely

controlled emotions were perking more violently than the coffee.

'How good it is to have you at the table with us, Everett.' Madame reached for her syllabub greedily. 'The meal is never complete when you are not present.'

Although Madame seemed impervious to the undercurrents, I knew that she had probably registered more than any of us. She had also cleaned her plate at every course with gusto and looked brighter and stronger for it.

'How good to enjoy my food without dear Richie at my elbow to warn me of the dietary hazards in every bite I take,' she said to me when the coffee and mints came round. 'Dr Anderson is refreshingly mute.'

I'd noticed that, but I couldn't say that anyone else had been exactly forthcoming. Lost in their own thoughts – or more probably schemes.

'No one to tell me how dangerous is caffeine.' Madame reached avidly for her cup. 'Nor how many hours of sleep I shall lose if I indulge in it.'

'Everett?' At the far end of the table, Monica raised an eyebrow. 'We're not having coffee in the drawing room?'

Everett shook his head; obviously we were not.

'A special treat tonight,' he announced. 'In the cinema. The latest Bollywood blockbuster – a little musical epic, for which I contributed some financial backing. It will première in Bombay in a fortnight, play most of the cinemas in the subcontinent, then selected cinemas in London and across Great Britain. But we are going to see it first tonight. I believe it's called a Sneak Preview.'

Only if it follows a major film in an ordinary commercial cinema – with audience reaction cards to be collected and assessed after the performance. This was obviously just the usual grovelling to a sponsor.

But who was I to correct him? He already had the audience reaction he wanted: a horrified recoil from people who had never seen a Bollywood musical and would cheerfully have paid good money *not* to have to watch this one.

But he was *their* sponsor, too – and they were trapped.

'Splendid!' Only Madame was enthusiastic. Caffeine-fuelled and good for the next few hours, she welcomed the prospect of something new and interesting to do. She reached eagerly for the wheels of her chair, ready to go.

'Let me.' I moved to the back of her chair and pulled her out from the table, then turned to Everett. 'Lead the way.'

He did so. Walking beside Madame and me, followed by the others, he took us down another corridor I had never seen and into a luxurious viewing room.

I was conscious of eyes – avid, hostile eyes – glittering from the shadows along our path. Shadow? Richie? Both? Exiled from the Presence, but jealously keeping watch.

Or possibly just a few of the minions, keeping track of us so that they could appear and dance attendance the instant Oversall might want them?

We had hardly settled into the deep comfortable arm-chairs than Gerta and a helper appeared with trays of brandy and liqueurs.

We made our selections and relaxed into the plush comfort as the lights dimmed, the curtains parted to reveal the screen, the tinkling music swelled . . .

J. Arthur Rank – eat your heart out.

The colour, the locale, the teeming hordes, the young vibrant lovers, the bright catchy music – we were swept away into an exotic magical world.

Pity about the plot – but you can't have everything.

At some point as the dizzying story swung along, I became aware that we were losing our audience.

'Headache . . .' a female voice murmured as a dark shape momentarily blotted out the screen and left the room.

'Me, too . . .' That sounded like Candy, making her escape.

'That maid with the fever . . . really should check on her . . .' There went Anderson, jumping ship – and avoiding another possible confrontation with me after the film.

The glorious hodge-podge of unlikely song and dance sequences and scenes that had never been vetted by a continuity girl continued to flash across the screen.

They were matched by the dark hunched shadows trying to depart inconspicuously, no longer bothering to make excuses, just sneaking out. It was like the old days in the theatre on the cruise ships when the weather began to worsen, the sea to heave and weak stomachs to churn.

At last the triumphant music swelled, the stars got as close to a clinch as the custom allowed and we had the fade out. The lights went up in the viewing room and I looked around to count the survivors.

Overall, Madame and me.

'I don't think they liked it,' Overall said.

'It was not made for them. It will be a great success,' Madame informed him firmly.

'Maybe –' I checked my watch – 'it's a bit long for European bottoms.' Three hours was rather overdoing it, but I gathered they like their money's worth on the subcontinent.

'No matter.' Overall shrugged. 'Advance bookings in India alone have covered production costs. It will show a profit, the only question is: how much?'

'Congratulations.' A sudden attack of envy prevented me from sounding whole-hearted. All the colour, flamboyance and vitality of the film had brought home to me what I was missing: my world. The theatrical world. I wanted to be part of it again.

But I had to stay here. For Nessa's sake.

Ironically, Overall was stepping into the world I wanted. Perhaps he was succumbing to nostalgia for his early days when he was cutting a swathe through café society. A throwback to the carefree time before the intrusion of the media and the demands of the shareholders had driven him into seclusion.

'*Umm-mm.*' Madame stifled a yawn, her caffeine fix was wearing off. She looked smaller, more vulnerable – and exhausted.

'I'll send for Richie.' Noticing, Oversall was instantly contrite. 'He'll take you home.'

'I think not!' Madame drew herself up. 'We are being observed – do you not feel it?'

Now that she mentioned it, I did. No one was in sight, not that that meant anything. Common sense told me that the staff would not slope off to bed while Oversall was still up and about. Silent, unobserved, there would be people all around us, but people who were basically indifferent. The hostility was elsewhere.

'After your performance at dinner,' Madame pointed out to Oversall, 'it may be expected that you will go with Vanessa – and remain for the night.'

'I'm not sure everyone will have noticed the wedding ring,' I demurred. Not that that had ever made any difference to Oversall.

'We shall both see Vanessa to her door,' Madame ordered. 'Then it will be necessary for you to take me to my own quarters. No one watching could question that.'

Chapter Twenty-Six

Madame was right. We were still observed.

From the moment we entered the cloister, the hairs on the back of my neck prickled. An unseen audience was out there, watching our every move.

Bud? Almost certainly. But . . . who else? Should I count Brutus?

'Later than I thought,' Oversall announced loudly, looking at his watch in an exaggerated gesture. He stepped forward, took the key from my hand and unlocked the door for me. 'We won't come in.'

'No,' Madame agreed. 'I am too tired.' She watched us severely, the picture of a suspicious chaperone. Playing to the gallery – both of them. Enjoying it, too, I suspected.

'Goodnight, then, and . . .' I paused in the doorway, bending my knees slightly so that I could look up at Oversall. 'And thank you. It's been a lovely evening.'

'There'll be many more.' He brushed my cheek with his lips. 'This is just the beginning.'

Madame cleared her throat meaningfully and he moved to the back of her chair, pausing only long enough to see me close the door.

Leaning against the door after I had locked it and thrown the bolt, I heard the sound of his footsteps fading as he wheeled Madame home.

Home. Oddly, this place was beginning to feel like that.

I kicked off my shoes and hurled myself down on the

sofa. Just for a minute. I was exhausted suddenly – the evening's performance had really taken it out of me.

And perhaps I shouldn't have had that last brandy . . .

I awoke abruptly, disorientated and uneasy, unsure of where I was – or why – and what had pulled me out of a deep dreamless sleep.

Slowly, it came back to me: where I was and why. But not what had disturbed me.

Perhaps it was the discomfort of the kaftan twisted around me or the turban that clung achingly tight to my head. Or perhaps it was the growing realization that it would be a very good idea to get up and go to the bathroom – and fast.

I shuffled into my shoes and stumbled off to attend to the necessary. On my way back to turn off the light in the living room before retiring to the bedroom to finish my night's sleep, I began to feel that something else was uncomfortably amiss.

I looked around groggily, trying to discover what – and trying not to wake myself up too fully to get back to sleep again.

Nothing . . . Something . . .

Then I heard it, and not for the first time. I recognized it as the sound that had pulled me out of slumber.

The piercing wail of a distressed feline.

'Duchess . . .?' I called. 'What's the matter? Gloriana . . .? Where are you? Come here . . . come on . . .'

No response. No bright little bundle of white fur emerged from the shadows to twine around my ankles and berate me for what was bothering her. Nothing.

Then a long agonized cry sounded again, like the wail of a siren. She was outside.

The guard dogs were running loose outside.

I charged to the door and wrenched it open.

'Duchess . . .?' Had she slipped past us when Oversall opened the door for me?

No. I would have noticed. I had been attuned to every nuance of that mocking scene we had played. Nothing had stirred except our unseen audience. Apart from which, the Duchess was an inside cat – and there had been strangers at the door. She would have retreated into the bedroom and waited for me to join her, not rushed out into the unknown.

But I hadn't seen her inside, either. In fact, I hadn't even thought about her. Guilt washed over me. Tired and half-sloshed, I had fallen asleep as soon as I stretched out on the sofa.

'Gloriana . . .? Duchess . . .?' I called frantically. 'Here, kitty, kitty . . .'

The answer was a shriek of pain, still in the distance. Why didn't she come to me? I had a frightening thought. Along with the guard dogs, did the gardeners set snares for moles or foxes or other pests? Was she caught in some kind of trap?

I stepped out into the cloister and peered into the darkness.

She gave that anguished cry again and I turned in the direction of it and saw her. She seemed to be suspended in space, a white bundle against the blackness of the Monk's robes, clutched in his merciless hands as he stood just outside his cell.

She was in a trap, all right – but the trap was for me.

'Put her down,' I said evenly. 'Let her go.'

There was another agonizing shriek as he twisted her tail with one hand. The other hand remained firmly around her throat.

He moved backwards a couple of steps, jerking his head in a silent command to go to him. At the same time, he did something to make the cat cry out again.

Now I knew why Nessa had followed the Monk.

And why I had to follow him, too.

I left my door open as I moved out into the cloister. Would

Brutus and Bud notice it? Or had they already completed their rounds for the night and gone off duty? If they did notice, what good would it do?

The figure ahead was moving in a strange crabwise progress. Afraid to turn his back on me?

Had Nessa tried to tackle him before? Was that why he was being so cautious?

In more ways than one. I drew close enough – only to be waved back to a more respectful distance – to see that the cat had been wrapped up in some restraining cloth, so that she couldn't defend herself with those strong legs and sharp little claws. Only the tail swung free – the better to be twisted – and the little head, which kept turning and stretching against the hand clamped tightly around her neck.

I ached to get my hands around *his* neck.

We were heading for that fake Gothic tower. Did he think the first attempt had been worth an encore? Or was it case of *If at first you don't succeed . . .?*

Ahead of me, the hooded figure stumbled, then recovered its balance. The bundle in its arms writhed and twisted, trying to escape. Good girl, she was going down fighting – we both were.

I moved closer while the Monk was regaining his footing and wrestling with the cat. Not much closer, but every little bit was an advantage.

As though he had caught my thought, he lifted his head and waved me back. He wasn't taking chances, I was as close as I was going to get.

After a moment, he sidled forward again, still watching me, still on guard. He signalled me to move again, but to keep my distance. We were nearly at the foot of the Gothic tower.

'Let her go.' I tried again. 'I'll come with you, but let the cat go.'

He gave a slow emphatic shake of the head. While he had the cat, he had me.

A cold wind swept across the greensward, rustling the

bushes and wrenching the few remaining leaves off the trees. Otherwise, there was silence all around us – no night noises, no dogs barking, no owl stirring. The moon was pale and unreliable, clouds scudded in front of it, blotting out what faint light it shed.

The Monk shuffled sideways a few more steps and waited for me to follow. We were coming up to the moat, on rougher terrain now, studded with large rocks and tussocks of marsh grass.

As I did, I stumbled and just saved myself from falling. I sensed a grim satisfaction emanating from the dark figure – he wanted me hurt.

'My ankle –' I decided to give him what he wanted – until I got close enough to give him what he deserved. 'I think it's sprained.'

He motioned me forward relentlessly and I managed a realistic limp. Wounded, weak, not much of a danger to him. But he was cautious, nonetheless.

He held up his hand, stopping me again. He had reached the door to the tower. He swung it open and stood well back, motioning me to go ahead. He wanted me in front of him now and not behind him, cutting off any retreat as we plodded up the circular stone staircase.

'It's so dark . . .' I hesitated. 'I can't see –'

The cat gave an anguished yowl. He was hurting her again.

I limped forward, almost tripping over the too-high doorstep, and felt my way up the uneven stone steps. I had reached the first narrow arrow-slit before I heard the foot-steps start up behind me. They moved more smoothly and confidently than mine, indicating familiarity with the territory. He probably knew his way blindfolded.

He let me keep well ahead of him. He was in no hurry. It was hours yet until dawn. He had enough time to dispose of me, dump the cat back where she belonged, replace the costume on the dummy of the monk in its cell and be back in his own life, the picture of innocence, when my body was discovered in the moat. Again.

I could see his plan clearly: *Poor Vanessa* – drawn back to the scene of her nearly fatal accident – and this time it *had* been fatal. What could have possessed her? Perhaps she'd had some sort of flashback to the accident in the night. Groggy and half-asleep, she had decided to follow it up, hoping it was the beginning of the return of her memory – if she could just catch it. But the night was dark, she was still weak, exhausted from a late night and the long stumbling trek to the tower and up all those winding stairs. Obviously, she had then had another dizzy spell when leaning over the parapet to look down at the moat. *Poor Vanessa . . .*

It could work. It was plausible enough. Someone had nearly got away with it the first time. This time . . . *Poor Vanessa.*

But who? And why?

Ivor? On the *If I can't have you, nobody can* principle? Unlikely. He would never have stood a chance in the first place – and he knew it. He was just a grubby little chancer who thought he could get away with manipulating a woman without a memory of her own. But was he furious enough at being thwarted to want revenge?

Anderson? There was – or could be – something there. I had felt it. But an ambitious man doesn't mess with the boss's woman. Only she hadn't been the boss's woman at first. Had he felt betrayed? Cheated? Made to look a fool? Only . . . he knew the truth about me. A truth that would be revealed in an autopsy – unless he conducted it himself.

Bud? Was that why no dogs were barking? Had he stashed Brutus away – and given permission for the other guards to take an early night? That could be checked – but who would bother? It was almost axiomatic that the person who discovered the body was the person the police investigated first and most closely. And Madame herself had noticed his interest in Nessa. Had Nessa been interested in him? As Head of Security, he was well placed to know information – and the secrets they would pay to learn. Was he the enemy within?

Shadow? His hostility was clear and uncomplicated. But how far would he dare to go in risking his father's wrath? Glowering and dumb insolence were just about his speed.

Richie? His motives were less clear. His devotion to Madame was undoubted, but Nessa posed no threat to her.

Or even *Oversall himself* – playing some sort of double game? No . . . slightly reluctantly, I had to exonerate Oversall. Those stairs alone would have had him wheezing by this time – but there was no sound from the Monk. He was someone younger and with better breath control.

I reached the top of the stairs – and the door leading out on to the parapet stood open. Waiting. I lurched through it and looked around, trying to get my bearings before the Monk appeared.

The walkway was about four feet wide – not much room to manoeuvre. The top of the tower rose another seven or eight feet above it, tapering to a blunt platform with just enough room for a brave piper or bugler to stand on while rallying the troops – and making a prime target of himself.

But it was all a fake, I reminded myself. Perpetrated by some mad Victorian industrialist and perpetuated by Oversall because it appealed to his warped sense of humour.

I turned away from the tower – to the sight I had been dreading: the outer wall with the long low openings that turned the parapet into a battlement. The openings where archers supposedly could stand to rain arrows down on invaders, from which boiling oil could be poured on insurgents trying to storm the tower.

I wondered from which opening Nessa had – not fallen, but been pushed. I closed my eyes momentarily against the vision of her spinning helplessly down, down, down into the moat.

There was a sudden rushing scrabbling noise behind me. I turned and opened my eyes.

The Monk hurtled through the tower door and out on to the roof. He moved quickly, positioning himself with his back against the tower and looked around. Now he *was* breathing heavily, I noticed.

He was also not so much in command as he had earlier appeared. He had obviously suspected that I might be waiting to ambush him, to rush at him when he reached the top and give him that fatal push that would send him tumbling down the stairs.

But I couldn't have done that: it might have hurt the Duchess.

While he held the cat, he held the ace of trumps.

He seemed to remember this. He turned towards me, his head lowered, his shoulders hunched, the picture of menace.

'So –' he said, his voice low and guttural. 'So now – you jump!'

Chapter Twenty-Seven

'Why?' I clasped my hands at my throat in the classic gesture of distress – which masked the long slide of the zipper that would allow me to throw off the kaftan for more freedom of movement. 'I don't understand.'

An implacable wave of his hand directed me to an opening of the battlement. It was reinforced by another pained yowl from the cat.

Sorry, Duchess, but I'm not taking the high jump. Not even for you. Hang in there.

She did better than that, she began to struggle again. Twisting, squirming, snarling, trying to bite, fighting to get a paw free. And keeping the Monk fully occupied trying to control her.

Go, girl, go! I cheered silently, moving closer while the Monk was distracted. I just needed to get close enough to –

'Halt!' He caught me. He raised one hand in the *Stop!* position, the other hand now grasped the cat by the scruff of her neck. The swathing cloth fell away, but she was immobilized by her position. Her eyes rolled, her ears and mouth twitched, but there was nothing else she could do.

He marched to the parapet and held her out over space.

'Now jump!' he ordered. 'Or I let go!'

Cats can fall from dizzying heights and survive. She had a better chance than I had. But I couldn't risk it – not and ever face Nessa again.

'But why?' I played for time. 'Why me? Why this? You owe me some explanation.'

'I owe you nothing!' he snarled.

'But I don't understand.' I spread my hands in a helpless gesture. 'Why? I . . . I don't want to die . . . without even knowing why . . .'

'Yes, yes,' he sneered. 'The famous amnesia, no?'

'No – Yes –' There was something off-key here – what? I cocked a professional ear: something wrong about the timbre of his voice. If I could keep him talking, I might be able to identify it.

'It's true. I remember nothing. Not even being up here before. Not you – not anything. Please –' I gave a sniff as pathetic as I could make it. 'I – I'll beg – if you want.'

'Yes – beg!' It had been the right thing to say. There was an unpleasant relish in his voice – and . . . something else.

But he had moved back from the parapet and the Duchess was no longer dangling over it. Her eyes met mine and her muscles tensed. I got the feeling we were both waiting our chance.

'Please –' I said. 'Just tell me why –'

'You are in the way!' The hooded head turned towards me, face hidden deep within the dark folds. I could feel the enmity surging out at me.

All that hatred. Shadow? Or someone else? The voice wasn't quite right for Shadow. How many enemies had Nessa made?

The moon was lost behind an increasing cloud cover and the wind was rising. It blew chill against my face and I could feel the hem of my kaftan stirring. The hem of the Monk's robe was moving, too; it was of a heavier material than the kaftan. It might not actually trip him, but it might impede his progress if the wind kept strengthening.

'Why?' I had to keep his attention on me. 'What ever happened? What drove you to this? I have no idea what I might have done, what I might have said.' I repeated the

213

argument that had incensed him earlier. 'You owe me an explanation!'

'I owe you nothing!' It worked. The murderous rage returned, he shook with it. 'You walked in here and took everything! *You* owe *me*! And now you will pay!'

'Tell me!' I demanded. As he moved towards me, I moved back, aware that he was edging me towards one of the openings.

'I tell you nothing! You will die as ignorant as you have lived.' He tensed to spring. 'You stupid, stupid woman!'

'Stupid – perhaps. Woman – no!' I yanked off my turban and hurled it at him.

There was a muffled shriek. The cat dropped to the stone floor as he instinctively raised both hands to fend off the unexpected missile.

I tore off the kaftan, swirling it like a bullfighter's cape at his ankles as he lunged forward.

Shriek? My mind registered it belatedly. I caught at the outstretched arms and was not now surprised to find my hands closing around slender wrists.

'Who *are* you?' the creature gasped, writhing in my grip.

'Who are *you*?' I countered, forcing the creature back against the tower wall. Without the reinforcement of terror and the unknown, it was weaker than I had imagined.

Then it gathered itself and made a desperate lunge against me, sending both of us stumbling towards the edge of the battlement.

But I was stronger. I forced it – her – back against the tower again. Something fell from the folds of her robe and clattered as it hit the stones.

She had begun gasping out little cries of distress. 'You are hurting me,' she sobbed.

'You were going to kill me! You tried to kill Nessa!' Fury swept over me, I pulled her away from the wall and shook her violently.

The cat hadn't run away. I was dimly aware of a white shape crouching by the door to the stairs, watching me with approval: that was the way to treat a rat!

I kept on shaking her, too furious to stop. The folds of the cowl flapped back and forth across her face until, finally, it fell back completely. A sudden burst of weak moonlight illuminated a pale face and hair that shone gilt.

'Yvonne!' Once I'd discovered that the Monk was female, I shouldn't have been surprised. Who else among them had the background to know about costumes, optical illusions, sound effects? I remembered the sound of her piano as I passed her quarters, leading me to assume she was inside – then finding her with Oversall. 'Yvonne!'

At our feet, the object that had dropped from her concealing robes gave a little preliminary cough and then the monks' choir rang out, chanting their rejection of the world and the glory of the spiritual life.

'You!' Her face contorted. 'You're not Vanessa! Who are you?'

'I'm Vance. Her twin. Her fraternal twin.'

'Twin? Not Vanessa! Then she *is* dead!' She gave a brief exultant laugh. 'I won!'

'No,' I said. 'Nessa won. She's still alive, she's getting better. And she's got me to look after her. And Oversall. But you're on your own – alone – and you're caught!' For a fleeting instant, I felt almost sorry for her.

'Oversall! Everett Oversall!' She spat the name out like a curse, beginning to struggle again. 'It's all *his* fault! I gave up everything for him! If it wasn't for him, I'd be famous now! Films, hit records, awards – he took it all away from me!'

Oh, yes. I'd heard it all before. From every tuppenny-ha'penny little no-hoper who'd ever managed to get a foot on the lowest rung of the ladder, but had abandoned all the effort of the long climb with relief the minute a wealthy meal ticket had come along. Of course, they then spent the rest of their lives berating the poor sucker for their lost careers.

Except that Oversall had never married Yvonne. He had married Nessa.

215

Jealousy! *The place reeks of it,* Madame had said. *Writhes with it.*

Yvonne was writhing now, trying to twist free of my grasp.

'Let me go!' she ordered. 'Vanessa is alive – you said so yourself. You have nothing to blame me for!'

'No?' I tightened my grip. 'What about Kiki? What about Francesca?'

'What about them? They were fools! They were in the way!'

'Only in your way.' But that was enough. She recognized no other.

'*Only!*' she shrieked. '*Only* me! You sound like Everett Oversall! He ignores me! Neglects me! He chases the newer ones now, the younger ones – I am just part of the wallpaper!'

'So you wanted revenge.' This was not the moment to correct her idiom. Those slender fingers were still curling and writhing dangerously – itching to claw my face off. Those strong clever fingers dancing over a piano keyboard would be equally adept tapping out instructions to a computer. Embezzling funds and transferring them to some secret account of her own; siphoning off vital information she could purvey to interested parties she had met while entertaining at Oversall's private little soirées. Not just for the money – for the revenge.

Yvonne – the enemy within. This was going to hit Oversall hard. Somehow, I didn't think Madame would be so surprised. I didn't think much of anything surprised Madame.

'Revenge – yes! Of course! Even now – when he returns his attention and his money to the theatre again – he never thinks of me! He invests in a play – and brings Vanessa here! He backs a stupid Bollywood film! What next? What? Anything – anyone – but me!'

'Easy –' I tried to calm her. 'Take it easy.' She was thrashing about so much I was afraid she was going to collapse on me. At the same time, I could see that she had

216

a valid point. If nothing else, my newly discovered brother-in-law was guilty of monumental tactlessness.

'*I* could have starred in that film! I have records that should be reissued. I can make new ones. My voice is still good –'

And loud. And getting louder by the minute. It was surprising that she hadn't roused half the household. She might yet.

'Damn Everett Oversall!' she shrieked. 'Damn him! He betrayed me! He betrayed you! He betrays everyone! Hell is too good for him!'

The cat gave a sudden corroborative yowl. I looked to see her moving away from the stairwell, her hackles rising, her tail bushed out. She met my eyes for a moment and flashed a warning.

She was right. I had been paying too much attention to what Yvonne was saying and not enough to what she was doing. Each fresh burst of abortive struggle had edged us closer to the parapet – and to one of the openings.

No wonder Dear Yvonne had been so forthcoming with her hatred and contempt. No matter that she had confessed. She had no intention of leaving me alive – male or female – to bear witness.

Male or female. The irony struck me and I laughed aloud.

'What is so amusing?' Offended and furious, she stopped struggling briefly and glared at me.

'You. Me. Us.' I swung her back towards the tower wall. 'Me, dressed as a woman. You, dressed as a man – and a monk, at that.'

'You are sick!' She renewed her struggle, but now I was conscious that she was deliberately trying to force us to the parapet again. 'Mad!'

One of us was mad, but it wasn't me.

Perhaps it would be better if I was. We'd be more evenly matched. She was fighting with the manic strength of the insane, whereas I was beginning to tire. It was taking all my energy just to hold her to a standstill. I didn't rate my chances of wrestling her down the narrow winding staircase and back to the main house.

The cat yowled again and I saw that she was now on the other side of us, perilously close to underfoot. Was she trying to help? *Trip her, Duchess, don't trip me!*

Yvonne suddenly realized the cat was there and began lashing out with her feet, trying to drop kick her over the parapet.

'No, you don't!' Fury gave me a surge of energy and I shook her violently again. Perhaps too violently. Her head snapped back and she went limp.

'Yvonne!' Instant guilt swept over me. Had I snapped her neck? Killed her? I relaxed my hold, and let go of one of her arms to have a hand free to turn her face towards me to assess the damage.

It was the oldest trick in the world – and I had fallen for it!

She sprang back into spitting snarling life. The arm I had foolishly released swung out, hand splayed, fingernails clawing for my eyes.

I tried to recapture the arm – or at least fend it off. At the same time, I tried to swing her sideways to keep those lashing out feet away from the Duchess.

Down beside our scuffling feet, the monks' chorus chanted on, their massed melodic voices rising and falling in the Latin devotions of centuries gone by.

The cat was backing away from the sound, looking from the recording to the tower door with equal distaste.

Get out of here! I tried to beam a message to her – cats were supposed to be telepathic, weren't they?

Maybe not this cat. She gave me a jaundiced look. I was being stupid again.

Yvonne was keeping me too busy to worry about it. I'd caught her arm, but she was kicking at me wildly, varied by an occasional knee thrust to the groin. I was beginning to tip off-balance.

Leave! I tried to reach the cat. *Now!* I wished I could.

I had my hands full – literally – with Yvonne and we were swaying too close to the edge again.

The cat looked from me to the tower door. Perhaps I was beginning to get through to her. Then her tail bushed out afresh and she backed towards the parapet. Her eyes grew huge and round as she stared at the door to the stairwell.

Over a sudden lull in the chanting, I heard a strange clicking scrabbling sound from the stairwell.

Yvonne had begun a low vicious monotone. I didn't understand French – which was probably just as well – but she was obviously cursing me thoroughly.

To hell with her, too! I kept watching the cat as her mouth opened in a snarl and she did some cursing of her own, drowned out as the chanting began to swell in volume. I followed her gaze to the tower door in time to see shadows moving there.

With something between a triumphant bark and a menacing growl, Brutus burst through it and out on to the walkway, Bud right behind him holding tightly to the other end of his leash, trying to keep him under control.

Yvonne and the cat both shrieked. Probably I did, too.

Brutus lunged forward and I let go of Yvonne. He and Bud could take over now. My concern was for the Duchess. I swooped her into my arms before Brutus could notice her.

Then it happened so fast I hardly had time to blink.

There was a final scream as Yvonne backed away from the charging Alsatian, overbalanced and fell from the aperture she had destined for me.

Brutus thrust his head through it and looked down, whining at being deprived of his prey. Bud moved forward and there was a clunk as his foot struck the monks' choir, sending it hurtling into the void after Yvonne as the voices rose in a crescendo.

There was a muted thud I didn't want to think about, followed by a distant clatter as the monks' voices were silenced for ever.

Silence. I clutched the Duchess and we buried our faces in each other's necks.

As from a great distance, I heard Bud say: 'Down, Brutus, down! Friends. Good boy. Sit!'

Then: 'I heard all that chanting, so I came to see what was up. And I heard screaming. Are you all right, Miss Vanessa?'

A comforting arm draped across my shoulders, an avuncular hand dropped to give my arm an encouraging squeeze – and froze when it encountered a firm bicep.

'Miss Nessa?' His voice faltered uncertainly. I raised my head and met his puzzled eyes.

'You're not Miss Va –'

'No,' I said. 'I'm not.'

Chapter Twenty-Eight

She was sleeping. Breathing smoothly and evenly, her colour almost back to normal, her hair growing back in short curly tendrils. The best sight I'd seen since I got back to England.

'I don't know when she'll wake up,' Dr Anderson warned. 'It's best to let her do so naturally. It may be some time.'

'That's all right.' I drew a chair up to the bedside and settled into it. 'I'll wait.'

'We also,' Madame said. Overall positioned her wheel-chair beside me and pulled up a chair for himself. All the next of kin.

'Well . . .' Anderson was in full disapproving medic mode, but unable to do anything about it since the entire private hospital belonged to Overall.

'You *do* realize –?' He was safer frowning at me and the offering in my arms. 'Most people bring flowers.'

'She'll be happier with this.' The room was already so crammed with flowers that it looked like a florist's shop.

'She will, indeed,' Overall said. The decisive word.

'Well . . .' Unsatisfactory, but Anderson obviously wanted to keep this job. 'I have other patients . . .' With an *On your heads be it* shrug, he left the room.

'Now.' I turned to face Overall. 'Are you going to tell me what's been happening?' I hadn't seen him for a couple of weeks, not since that nightmare night when he had been brought to stand looking down at Yvonne's broken body and think his own thoughts.

'There isn't much to tell.' His face shuttered. 'Everything has been taken care of.'

Swept under the carpet with the golden broom, he meant.

'Yvonne was with us for a very long time.' Madame did not look at him. 'We have returned her to her native France. Her family were satisfied with the arrangements. They were generous. My nephew will . . . notice her absence.'

'I see.' I did. Generous arrangements – and the family would also have been made aware that a major scandal about Yvonne was being covered up. No wonder they were satisfied. And it was Aunt Madame, was it? I filed that one away for later contemplation.

'And Kiki?' I asked. 'I suppose you shipped her back to her family, too?'

'We did everything necessary, everything possible. They, also, were – not happy, but satisfied with the arrangements.'

As they say, money can't buy happiness, but it can certainly make misery more comfortable.

'Francesca –' Oversall said heavily, before I could enquire about her. 'We still don't know. We have no idea where the body is hidden. It's . . . unfortunate that you didn't find out from Yvonne what she did with her.'

'Sorry to be so incompetent,' I said. 'But I was fighting for my life at the time.'

'Do not be angry.' Madame leaned over and put her hand on my arm. 'It is over now.'

Was it? I wondered if Oversall thought so.

The cat stirred in my arms. She had been staring from the motionless figure on the bed to me and back again for some time. Now she wanted to get closer to investigate.

I set her down gently on the side of the bed and she crept forward delicately, nose twitching.

We all watched her with varying degrees of gratitude. There was nothing left to say – and it was something to occupy us.

Closer and closer she moved, until the cold wet nose

touched Nessa's cheek. Nessa smiled in her sleep and instinctively stretched out a hand. The cat curled into it. Nessa's smile widened and her eyelids fluttered open. As I had noticed myself, it was a lovely way to be awakened.

'Glori –' she whispered. Her eyes opened the rest of the way and she saw me. 'Gloriana –'

'Both your Glorianas,' I said. 'Although she strikes me as more of a Dowager Duchess.'

'You think so?' Her eyes began to shut again. The cat stretched out beside her and began purring loudly, no longer concerned that there seemed to be two of us.

'What . . .?' She was fading. 'I . . . doing here?'

'Just rest.' Overall rose to hover over her protectively. 'You're safe now.'

'Everett . . .' She greeted him faintly, there seemed to be genuine affection in her smile. She looked beyond him. 'And Madame . . .' There was affection for her, too.

'Go back to sleep,' Madame said. 'All is well.'

'Is it?' She looked wildly at me for a moment, struggling for something she ought to remember. 'Vance – have I missed your Opening Night?'

'No, I haven't got a show yet. I've been . . . side-tracked.'

'Don't worry.' Overall was back to speaking with his usual assurance. 'We'll find something for him to do.'